Ever since **Lisa Childs** at age eleven (a Mills & all she wanted was to b over forty novels published with Mills & Boon, Lisa is living her dream. She is an award-winning, bestselling romance author. Lisa loves to hear from readers, who can contact her on Facebook, through her website, lisachilds.com, or at her snail-mail address, PO Box 139, Marne, MI 49435, USA.

If you liked *Legal Seduction*, why not try

A Week to be Wild by JC Harroway
Off Limits by Clare Connelly
Ruled by Anne Marsh

Discover more at millsandboon.co.uk

LEGAL SEDUCTION

LISA CHILDS

MILLS & BOON

First Published in Great Britain 2018
by Mills & Boon, an imprint of HarperCollins*Publishers*
1 London Bridge Street, London, SE1 9GF

© 2018 Lisa Childs

ISBN: 978-0-263-93206-5

MIX
Paper from
responsible sources
FSC C007454

This book is produced from independently certified FSC™ paper
to ensure responsible forest management.
For more information visit www.harpercollins.co.uk/green.

Printed and bound in Spain
by CPI, Barcelona

For my husband, Andrew Ahearne, who dared me to step outside my comfort zone of the area where I grew up and spent most of my life.

Moving with you has been an adventure and a reward.

Love you so much!

CHAPTER ONE

FOUR GLASSES, LIFTED HIGH, clinked against each other. Champagne bubbles foamed over the rims and streaked down the stems of the flutes.

"Cheers to Street Legal," Simon Kramer said, pride for the firm overwhelming him. Sixteen years ago, as a teenage runaway, he'd never thought he would go from living on the streets to owning them.

"Cheers to us," Ronan, one of Simon's law partners, said with a grin as he clinked his glass against theirs again.

"Cheers to you, Trev," Stone said to Trevor, who'd just won the biggest case their practice had ever had. And the four of them had had some damn big cases since graduating law school and starting their practice eight years ago.

After this win, they could close the doors of Street Legal and live off the settlement. But Simon knew that the others were like him: too young and too ambitious to stop achieving. And yet Simon wanted to make sure they took the time to enjoy their victories. So he'd talked his partners into leaving the office to celebrate at the new bar around the corner, The Meet Market.

This victory was especially sweet because Trev had won despite the opposing counsel getting their hands on information from the case files. Simon, as the managing partner, had put a plan in place so that would *not* happen again. If the mole was in their office, he would find it and *crush* it.

Trevor murmured, "I still want to know how the hell Anderson got his hands on that scientist's report."

"Don't worry about it," Simon said. He'd also set up this celebration because they all needed to blow off some steam. Or get blown...

Ronan glanced away from the women he'd been ogling to agree. "Don't give it another thought. It's not like we have a leak in our office, not with Simon doing all the hiring. Nobody can sniff out a con like a con. And our managing partner is the ultimate con."

Instead of being offended, Simon grinned. He wouldn't have survived had he not come up with money-making schemes for himself and for these guys. His friends had once been runaways, too. Simon had been running cons long before he'd met them.

"No, it's more likely Trev brought home some hottie who, after he rolled over and fell asleep, copied the case files he brought home," Ronan said.

Simon laughed. "You guys fall asleep?"

He couldn't sleep with anyone else around. He

wouldn't have survived on the streets if he'd trusted just anyone. Only these guys passed his test. They'd survived the streets together. Hell, they'd thrived. They had more money, fancier homes, faster cars and hotter women than any of them could have imagined having.

"I wish that's what happened," Trev said. "But this damn case put a hell of a crimp in my love life."

"That's why I thought we should check out this new bar," Simon admitted. Trying to figure out who was the mole had put a crimp in his sex life, too.

The Meet Market was exactly what it boldly claimed to be: the hookup hub of Midtown Manhattan. All the beautiful people were here: models, actors and actresses, designers...

And them. The most successful and notorious lawyers in the whole damn city.

Simon clinked his glass against Trevor's. "You won the case, so forget about it. Have some fun."

Trevor grinned. "I plan on it. But Ronan's right. We need to be careful about who we bring home or at least around our files."

Stone nodded in agreement. "Yes, because if word gets out that anything got leaked to the opposing counsel, we'll need to hire that damn PR firm to help with our image."

Since the age of social media, most cases were tried before they ever made it to court, which was why they routinely used a PR firm to help sway the public the way they wanted them swayed. To their side, of course.

Ronan chuckled. "Like there's any helping our image…"

They were known for being ruthless—in the courtroom and the bedroom. They all had a reputation for winning, by whatever means necessary. But in Simon's opinion, that was a cause for pride, not damage control.

"We're fine, guys," Simon assured his partners. "I got this." He gestured at the women around them. "Now, let's get one of them…"

"Just one?" Ronan asked with a grin as he watched a blonde walk past him, tossing her long, curly mane over her shoulder. Before heading after her, he slapped Trevor on the back. "Want me to see if she has a friend for you? Si's right. You need to relieve some stress after winning that case."

Trevor glanced across the room at a redhead. "I don't need your help." He blew out a ragged breath. "But I do need to relieve some stress."

Stone bumped Simon's shoulder with his. "Looks like Si here could use some help."

Ronan snorted. "Si needs no one's help when it comes to women. He's the worst womanizer of the four of us."

Simon didn't know whether that was a compliment or insult. Coming from the notorious divorce lawyer, it was probably a compliment. But before he could ask, Ronan hurried after the blonde who'd paused in the doorway, waiting for him to follow her.

"You know, I haven't seen *you* with anyone for a while," Stone said to him.

Simon shrugged. "I've been busy." Setting up trusts, drawing up contracts, setting his trap. But he was worried those were just excuses, not the real reasons.

He glanced around the bar and recognized some of the models from the billboards in Times Square and some of the actresses from plays. But nobody had his pulse quickening. He knew he could bring any one of them home with him or, as Ronan suggested, two. And maybe that was it. There was no challenge. No thrill of the hunt...

Just easy prey.

Like the redhead waving at Trevor from across the bar.

"Go," Simon urged him.

"Yeah," Stone agreed. "She's a hell of a lot prettier to celebrate your victory with than we are."

"Speak for yourself," Simon said, feigning offense.

With his thick blond hair and bright blue eyes, he'd been told he was better-looking than the hottest male movie stars—which was why he knew he could get anybody in the place to go home with him, even if he were still the broke runaway he'd once been.

Stone laughed, then said, "I may need to have

you sit at the table with me for some of my upcoming trial—to sway the jurors like you did for Trev."

"Hey, guys, you're going to have to start working out, so you can be your own jury eye candy," Simon said, his lips tugging up into a teasing grin. "I've got work of my own to do. So damn much money to manage."

Now it wasn't just his clients' but theirs, too. That probably mattered more to Simon than it did the others. But they hadn't grown up like he had—when the only money he'd known had always really belonged to other people.

"Hey, we sway most of the women jurors ourselves," Trevor stated with pride and a trace of defensiveness. "We just need you to sway the ones who like pretty boys."

Simon suppressed a laugh of amusement. He didn't want Trevor to know how funny he was, so he acted offended and replied, "Fuck you."

Trevor shook his head. "Sorry, man, you're not my type. Now, that redhead…" He sauntered off toward the woman.

Stone peered around the bar. "I better find someone, too, or I might wind up going home with you."

"You wouldn't get so lucky," Simon said as Stone headed off. Simon glanced around the bar now, too. It wasn't that he didn't want to be the only one going home alone. Or it wasn't *just* that. He needed a diversion, something to get his mind off the mole in their office.

He couldn't have been conned into hiring someone who would betray them. No. Like Ronan said,
there was no conning a con. His trap wasn't going
to catch anyone because the leak couldn't be in their
office.

So he wouldn't let it get to him. Not anymore.
He'd find someone else to focus all his attention on
for a little while. He wasn't into blondes like Ronan
was. And he'd learned the hard way that redheads
were nothing but drama. He needed to find a classy
brunette, someone who would actually pose a worth-
while challenge to his charm.

Before he could even look, his cell began to vi-
brate in his suit pocket. It wasn't a call but the tell-
tale buzz of a 911 text. Did any of the guys need his
help? He visually located them all in the crowded
bar, but they were totally engaged on the women
they'd found. Not one seemed in need of a wingman.

Simon pulled out the cell and cursed when he read
the screen. Damn it. His trap had been sprung. Someone was entering the office after hours, and there
was probably only one reason for that. Shoving the
cell back into his pocket, he hurried toward the exit.

But before he could leave, Trevor blocked his
escape. "What is it? Everything okay?"

It sure the hell wasn't, but he forced a grin. "Just
got a sext." From the security system. "I have to go."

Trevor chuckled. "Of course you wouldn't even
have to work for it." With an envious sigh, he stepped
aside to let Simon past.

He hurried out, aware that Trev wasn't the only one watching him. Let the guys think he was anxious to get naked. He would explain later. Right now he hoped to catch their mole in the act of copying active case files. The office was just around the corner.

The person had the security code, so no alarm had gone off, and no warning was sent to building security or the police station. Within moments he stepped off the elevator onto their floor, which was eerily silent and dark. The only light spilled from under the door of an office—*his* office.

He silently crossed the lobby, which had glass interior walls with hardwood floors. The exterior walls were the exposed brick of the old building. The ceilings were open to the ductwork and the rafters, the wood painted black while the copper pipes and steel ductwork gleamed in the dark.

Why the hell was the mole in *his* office? Had they graduated from selling secrets to stealing money? The door was ajar, the crack wide enough that he was able to peer through it.

Someone leaned over his desk, lush curves pressed against the black fabric of a tight skirt. His pulse quickened as he recognized that remarkable ass. He'd been discreetly admiring it for the past two years. He couldn't have afforded to be obvious about it, not with what a sexual harassment case could have cost the firm. And she had certainly never returned his interest. Now he knew why. She hadn't wanted sex. She wanted money.

Anger coursed through him, making his pulse race even faster. In addition to being incredibly sexy, Bette Monroe was cunning. She'd conned the ultimate con.

"What the hell are you doing?"

Bette jumped and the pen she'd been holding slipped from her grasp, rolled across the oak desktop and dropped onto the hardwood floor. She pressed her hand over her madly pounding heart before turning toward the door. When she saw her boss standing there, her heart beat even faster and not just because he'd startled her.

Seeing Simon Kramer was always a shock to a woman's system. With his golden-blond hair and piercing blue eyes, chiseled features and a muscular body, he was so beyond handsome that it wasn't even fair—to women or to other men. The other lawyers in the Street Legal law practice were good-looking but nowhere near as attractive as Simon. And not one of them wore a suit as well as he did even though they all had them tailor-made. Simon's was a silvery gray with a faint sheen of blue that brought out that startling blue of his eyes.

His voice a deep rumble, Simon asked, "What are you doing here?"

Realizing it was the second time he'd asked, albeit nicer this time, heat rushed to her face. She must have been staring at him like a fool. That was why she always made a point of never looking directly at him. His good looks were like a solar eclipse, staring too closely could cause blindness.

Maybe that was why her eyesight had gotten poorer in the two years she'd worked for Street Legal as Simon Kramer's executive assistant. She'd been standing too close to the sun. Her hand trembling, she shoved her thick frames farther up her nose. Since she only needed the glasses for reading, her distance vision blurred, and she couldn't see him as clearly now.

Until he stepped away from the door and strode across his expansive office to her. He leaned down so his face was close to hers. His eyes usually sparkled with amusement because he was always teasing his partners, his clients or other office employees. Never her, though. He only talked to her to give her orders. But when he did that, his eyes had never appeared like they did now—cold and hard like shards of blue ice.

She shivered.

"This is the last time I'm going to ask you," he said, "what the hell you're doing in my office."

More heat rushed to her face, and she stammered, "I—I was—"

"Looking for me?" he asked with one golden brow arching with skepticism.

"No," she admitted. She hadn't wanted to see him—not again—not since catching a glimpse of him in that new bar around the corner. Seeing him there—in that meat market—had confirmed she was doing the right thing. Just like her friends had been encouraging her, she needed to leave Street Legal.

It was too hard to work here, and especially too hard to work for *him*. Fortunately, she no longer needed this job.

"I was actually hoping *not* to see you," she said. When she'd noticed him and his partners walk into the bar, she'd been quick to leave, so he wouldn't see her there with her friends. She'd always been very careful to keep her private life private from everyone else at the firm. Most especially from him.

He sucked in a breath as if she'd struck him. "I'm surprised you'd admit that."

"I'm sorry," she said. "I didn't mean that the way it sounded." Which had been rude. Too bad she was such a lightweight that one glass of wine had lowered some of her inhibitions. Like now, when she looked at him again and heat rushed through her body. His eyes were so blue. Why did he have to be so good-looking?

"What do you mean, Bette?" he asked. "Why are you here? You need to give me an answer."

She drew in a shaky breath. "This is why I came when I knew you wouldn't be here," she said. "I didn't want to be caught."

"Damn it," he cursed. "I didn't expect this from you—of all of Street Legal's employees."

She could understand that. Some people, ambitious people, would kill to work at Street Legal. Other people—like her—didn't want to be associated with such an unscrupulous firm. Two years ago she'd had no choice; she'd needed money to be able to live in the city and to pay back her student loans. Now she had a choice. She reached for the note she'd left—unsigned—on his desk. Her name was just a line across the bottom.

"I'm sorry," she said again, and with her hand trembling, she passed the letter to him.

He glanced down at the paper. As he began to read it, his brow furrowed. He must have been confused because he murmured, "What the hell is this?"

Her heart continued to beat fast and hard. "It's—it's my letter of resignation." Which she had hoped to leave on his desk without running into him. Of course he would show up. Over the past two years there had been no escaping Simon Kramer. He even showed up in her dreams—dreams that left her with tight nipples and a pulsing clit. Not that she had a crush on him or anything.

In fact, there was very little she liked about Simon Kramer, except how he looked. But that was more a curse than a blessing—for her and all the weak-willed females he'd seduced. Not that he would seduce her or even try. She'd seen the women he dated: models and actresses—beautiful women. He had no interest in her. Just as she never looked at him, he never looked at her, either.

He shook his head. "I don't understand." And his brow was still furrowed with confusion. "Why are you quitting?"

She'd kept the resignation letter short and sweet. *This is official notice of my resignation. My last day of employment will be...*

Two weeks from now. Or hopefully sooner if he got mad and just fired her, and that was what she was hoping for. She doubted anyone had ever dumped Simon Kramer before—personally or professionally.

Thank you for the opportunity.

Thanks but no, thanks. She wanted no part of Street Legal anymore. No part of their high-profile cases. No part of sending flowers to their jilted lovers. No part of fielding the pleading calls from those same lovers.

She hadn't said any of that, though. She'd given no reason for leaving—because she hadn't had to.

So predictably he asked, "Why?"

Nonconfrontational by nature, Bette could only shrug. She was the one who apologized when someone else bumped into her on the street or jostled her on the subway. And that wasn't just the manners instilled with her Midwestern upbringing.

"You must have a reason." He persisted.

She had several. But she only shook her head. Her hair, which was so heavy, pulled at the knot that had slipped to the back of her head. The pins shifted, sticking into her skull. If she'd been home, she would have pulled them out, let down her hair.

But she couldn't do that around him. The tight bun—the glasses—that was her armor to protect herself around him. Not that he would make untoward advances. She knew even with her hair down and glasses off, she wasn't his type. But she felt more protected in her office camouflage. So that he wouldn't know the real her. Only her most trusted friends knew the real her. And she would never trust Simon Kramer.

"If you had no reason to leave," he said, his deep voice husky with frustration, "you wouldn't be leaving." He crumpled the letter in his fist.

And Bette's pulse leaped with fear. Although she was well aware of Simon Kramer's ruthlessness, she had never been afraid of him before. He'd never been warm and fuzzy with her, but he'd never been mean, either.

"I—I just want to leave," she said. And she wasn't talking only about his employ. She wanted to leave his office, too. But he stood in the path between her and the doorway.

He shook his head. "No."

"But—but you can't refuse my resignation..." Could he? Before deciding to leave the firm, she'd read over the employment contract he'd had her sign when he'd hired her, and she'd seen nothing about not being able to quit. But he was the contracts and trusts lawyer. He was the one who would have come up with the clauses and legal jargon that would make it possible for him to legally enslave someone.

"I can change your mind," he said, and even though his lips curved into a smile, his eyes remained cold and hard. "How much will it take?"

"You think this is about money?" Street Legal paid all their employees very well. That was why she'd come to work for him although she'd really wanted to work in a fashion house. But after interning at fashion houses, she knew how little they paid and how hard she would've worked.

He tilted his head, and his blue eyes narrowed as he studied her face. "Isn't everything about money?"

Maybe it was the wine that made her less censored than she would have ordinarily been but she admitted, "Unfortunately it is—to most people."

"Are you saying you aren't one of those people?" he asked, and one of his golden brows arched in skepticism. But there was more than skepticism in his eyes. He was looking at her a certain way that he never had before, a way that had nerves swimming in her stomach. He was actually *looking* at her, and there seemed to be an appreciation in his gaze as if he liked what he saw.

Damn. She was such a lightweight. She had to be drunk to imagine that Simon Kramer would look at her *that* way, like he wouldn't mind seeing more of her—*naked*.

"I wouldn't have taken the job working here if money didn't matter to me," she admitted. But having him to look at, to fantasize about, had given her the inspiration to succeed at her other job.

"So then more money will get you to stay," he said dismissively, as if he'd closed a case. He tossed her crumpled-up resignation letter into the brass trash can sitting beside his desk.

Frustration—and not just with this conversation—overwhelmed her, overcoming her natural inclination to avoid confrontation, and she blurted out, "No!"

Working for him these past two years had increased her frustration because of all those damn fantasies he'd inspired.

"But you just said—"

"I took the job because I needed money," she said. "I needed money *then*."

His eyes narrowed more as he studied her face. "And you don't need it now?"

"My reason for leaving has nothing to do with money," she said. Had she not found another source of income, she would have been forced to stay, but he didn't need to know that.

"So you do have a reason."

He wasn't the trial lawyer of their partnership, but he could have been. She felt like she was being cross-examined on the witness stand. And she didn't enjoy it one bit. Quitting was not a crime.

"I don't have to give you a reason." At least she didn't think she did.

Maybe she should have had a lawyer look at that employment contract before she'd written her resignation letter. But no matter how much she paid, no lawyer would be as good as Simon Kramer. He was the best.

And, according to his ex-lovers, not just at the law...

"Why don't you want to tell me?" he asked, and he stepped closer now, so close that she could feel the heat of his body through his suit and her cardigan and skirt.

Heat flushed her body, making her skin tingle. She tried to step back but the desk stopped her, the hard wood pressing into the backs of her thighs as he nearly touched the front of her. Her breasts pushed against the front of the gray cardigan as she struggled for breath. She had never been this close to him before. It was more than unsettling. Her knees trembled and her already tripping pulse quickened even more.

"Because it's personal," she murmured. And they had never been anything but businesslike with each other, except in her dreams.

He leaned down, so close that his warm breath whispered across her lips as he asked, "Are you in love with me?"

CHAPTER TWO

HER MOUTH HAD fallen open with the same shock Simon had seen on her face when he'd first caught her in his office. So he repeated his question, like he'd had to repeat his first one. "Are you in love with me?"

Color rushed to her face again. But she wasn't embarrassed. She was amused because she started laughing. Hers was no flirty, girlish giggle, either. Her laugh was deep and husky and had his pulse racing with attraction even as his pride bristled.

Focused on his face, her dark eyes widened. "You're serious? You think I'm in love with you?"

"No," he said, and his face heated a little with embarrassment. But it wouldn't have been the first time someone had fallen for him without any encouragement from him. "I don't."

Not anymore. Not after her reaction.

Apparently, it was a good thing he'd never acted on the attraction he'd felt for her. He had no doubt she might have sued for harassment. But now that she'd already given her notice…

"Then why would you ask...?" She trailed off as her voice cracked with the threat of another giggle. It turned into a hiccup instead.

He caught the faint scent of wine on her breath and asked, "Have you been drinking?"

"What does that have to do with anything?" she countered. "It's after office hours, and I'm not working. It doesn't matter how much I've had to drink."

"It does if it's affecting your judgment," he replied.

Just how affected was her judgment? He wasn't thinking about just tonight or about just the drinking. Other things could affect judgment. Like greed. Or some other kind of coercion. Maybe she had a lover at an opposing law firm. Had something like that affected her judgment enough that she'd sold information from their case files?

Was that why she didn't need money any longer?

He had to find out. Right now was probably his best chance—if she'd had enough alcohol to bring down her defenses. He had never seen Bette like this before. Or maybe he'd just never let himself see her like this—except for a stolen glance or two at her assets.

Simon hadn't been able to stop himself from admiring the lush curves of her hips and ass in her pencil-slim skirts. And the little cardigans she wore did nothing to hide the fullness of her breasts. They strained the buttons at the front, showing little glimpses of the lace camisoles she wore beneath the sweaters.

"So you think the only reasons I could have for wanting to quit are because I'm drunk or in love with you?" she asked, a smile curving her full lips.

Since she didn't usually look at him, he'd never noticed before how full her lips were—so full that she had a slight dimple in the middle of her bottom one.

He wanted to tug at that lip—with his lips and with his teeth. He wanted to nibble on it until she gasped for breath. Then he wanted those lips to touch him, to close around his cock as she sucked him deep into her throat.

His heart slammed against his ribs as desire sneaked up on him. This was Bette, his boring assistant. Except that she didn't want to be his assistant anymore.

So what did that make her? The spy who'd betrayed their practice? Simon needed to know for certain if she was the office mole. But how the hell was he going to get her to talk?

She wouldn't even give him the reason she was resigning. Why didn't she want him to know? What was she hiding?

In order to get her talking, he needed to talk first. The best way for a con to gain the confidence of his mark was to share a confidence of his own.

"I've always had a problem keeping assistants," he admitted to her. It wasn't exactly a deep, dark confession, but it was the truth. "You've lasted much longer than anyone else has." About a year and a half longer than her longest-working predecessor.

"I know people who would love to work for you."

He sighed. "For the wrong reasons. Professionally, they want to get ahead." They wanted to use the position as his assistant to launch their own legal careers.

Or they wanted to give him head. He wouldn't mind if Bette had wanted to do that, but that obviously wasn't why she'd taken the position as his assistant. She had never once showed any interest in him. Until now. "Or, personally, they want me."

Her eyes widened again, and so did her pupils, dilating as she stared up at him through the lenses of her black-framed glasses. The glasses were too big for her delicately featured face, which was probably why they kept sliding down her small nose.

"I—I don't want you..." she murmured, but there was no amusement in her voice now. Not even a hint of laughter. But her voice had grown more husky, and her pulse quivered visibly, erratically, in her long, slender neck.

He leaned even closer, so his lips just brushed over hers as he whispered, "Liar..."

She gasped, which moved her lips against his. He took advantage of her open mouth and deepened the kiss. First, he nibbled on her lips, like he'd wanted. Then he slid his tongue between them, into the sweet heat of her mouth. Would her body feel the same?

Hot and wet? He wanted to find out.

He clutched the back of her head in one hand, his fingers closing over that knot of soft, thick hair. It tickled his palm, making his skin tingle. The sensation surprised him. This was Bette, his assistant. She wasn't supposed to make his skin tingle or his cock swell and throb behind the fly of his dress pants.

But she was…

And it was…

His body pulsed and ached. He wanted her aching for him, too. So he moved his other hand, the one not in her hair. He slid it over the curve of her hip down her thigh to the hem of her skirt. He wanted to lift it, wanted to skim his fingers up the inside of her thigh to the heat of her core. But how drunk was she?

He didn't want to take advantage if she'd had too much to drink. And he suspected that she had because she was kissing him back, her tongue chasing his into his mouth. He tasted the wine on her tongue, crisp and slightly sweet. He wasn't surprised that she would drink a sweet and fruity white. She wasn't sophisticated like the women he usually dated.

Not that he wanted to date her. All he wanted was the truth. Why was she leaving? And was she the one who'd sold their secrets to opposing counsel?

At least that was all his mind wanted. His body was making demands of its own. And he found himself giving in to temptation. He moved his hand beneath her skirt, stroking his fingertips up the inside of her thigh.

She wore stockings, but they stopped halfway between her knees and her core. His finger touched lace and silk. She was wearing a garter?

He never would have thought Bette was the type to wear sexy underwear, let alone lingerie. His breath caught as he touched bare skin, which was even silkier than the stockings and the garter.

But the stockings and garter excited the hell out of him, too. Was she hiding something else—something super sexy—beneath that cardigan?

He moved his hand from her hair down the nape of her slender neck, then around her throat. Her pulse beat madly beneath his fingertip. She was as excited as he was.

He traced his finger lower, over her collarbone to the first button of that sweater. He flicked it open and then moved down to the next and the next, revealing the deep valley of her cleavage. She wasn't wearing a camisole, like he'd thought. She wore a red lace bustier adorned with tiny bows.

A garter and bustier?

His breath escaped in a ragged groan. Who knew Bette Monroe was so damn sexy and sensual? He'd had no idea.

Did someone else? Had she worn this lingerie because she was meeting someone? At the moment he didn't care. He didn't care about anything but the desire burning him up. His cock pulsed with excitement and the need for release. A release only Bette could give him...

She gasped and trembled against him. Then she

tensed. And her hands pressed against his chest, pushing him back.

"I—I..." she stammered. Her face was flushed with color, and her eyes glittered behind the lenses of her glasses.

"You want me," he finished for her.

She shook her head and her hair tumbled down around her shoulders. He'd loosened the pins, which fell onto the hardwood floor. Her hair was long, so much longer than he'd realized. It reached nearly to her waist. And it was thick and wavy. How had he never noticed how damn sexy it was? How damn sexy she was?

"I want to leave," she said, her voice steadier now as if she'd forced herself to stop stammering.

He stepped back and swept his arm toward the door. "Go ahead." He'd never had to hold a woman against her will. Usually he was the one who had to fight to escape.

Bette moved forward but swayed slightly. Maybe she'd had more to drink than he'd thought, which was another good reason to stop. Because despite what she claimed, she wanted him. He could easily change her mind about staying with just another kiss, another caress...

And he was tempted to do just that because he wanted her, so much that it surprised him. She could have betrayed his and his partners' practice. She could be a con, like him, like his father. Maybe the cardigan sweater and black-framed glasses were just part of the act and the lingerie was the real her.

Was that why he was suddenly attracted to her, because he hadn't had a challenge in so long? Bette Monroe might pose his greatest challenge yet. He watched as she walked toward the door, watched her hips rock back and forth beneath that tight, sexy skirt. And he swallowed a groan of desire.

Then she stopped, halfway to the door, and turned back to him and said, "I won't be coming back."

He arched a brow. "Really?"

"I am not working out a two-week notice," she said, and her voice wasn't just steady. It was dead calm with determination.

He grinned at the challenge she was going to pose. Then he told her, with equal determination, "Yes, you are."

She shook her head, tumbling all that glorious dark hair around her shoulders and over the cardigan. The thick tresses hid some of the red bustier he'd revealed. He'd always been a sucker for brunettes.

Had she known that? Was that why she'd interviewed to be his assistant two years ago? Had she been working him all this time?

"No," she said. "I can't work with you *now.*"

He shrugged. "Why not? Because I kissed you?" He intended to do a hell of a lot more than that to her. Over and over again. Now he wanted to see what was beneath that lingerie. He wanted to touch and taste every inch of her silky skin.

She nodded. "That's sexual harassment."

"You already turned in your resignation," he reminded her. It was probably a fine line, but he was a damn good lawyer. His employment agreements were indisputable. "And you will serve out your notice, just as stipulated in your contract."

"But—but…" Her mouth fell open on a gasp. "You can't want me to work here still."

Knowing that she was probably the mole, no, he shouldn't want her to work at Street Legal a second longer. But he would be careful to keep her away from all the case files.

He had other plans for keeping her busy. His body throbbed as some of the images he intended to act out flashed through his mind. Her on her knees, sucking on his cock.

Her sexy bare ass bent over his desk as he drove himself inside her…

Sweat broke out on his lip as tension gripped his body. He intended to sensually torment and seduce her into revealing her betrayal. But all of the thoughts of how he would do that were torturing him.

"Oh, I intend to work you," he warned her as he stepped closer to her. His chest bumped against her breasts, which rose with her pants for breath so much that they nearly spilled over the top of the bustier. "Long and hard…"

And that was just him.

She gasped again, and her dark eyes widened even more with shock. And that desire she kept denying.

"You can't make me do anything but work," she insisted, her voice husky and breathless.

He nodded but a grin tugged at his lips. "We'll see..."

She had no idea how persuasive he could be. He had never turned his charm on her before. But he fully intended to do that now.

He was going to seduce the office mole. He was going to con the con until she revealed all her secrets and begged to stay with him—in the office and in bed.

It was just a dream. That was all it had been. It couldn't have actually happened last Friday night. Simon Kramer couldn't have really hit on her.

On Bette Monroe.

He hadn't kissed her, hadn't touched her...hadn't hinted at wanting to do even more to her.

No. It was just a dream. And convincing herself of that was the only way she'd managed to come in to the office on Monday morning. That and that damn contract she'd signed. She had no doubt that he would enforce it had she decided to not work out her two-week notice.

The elevator bell dinged as the car reached the top floor. When the doors slid open, she sucked in a deep breath—bracing herself before she stepped out onto the floor for the Street Legal law practice. It was just two weeks. She'd lasted two years working for Simon Kramer, which—by his own admission— was longer than most of his previous assistants had.

Two weeks was nothing.

She lifted her chin and forced a smile for the receptionist as she walked past him on her way to her office. Miguel nodded in return. The former gang member looked more like a bouncer than a receptionist, which was appropriate since he often had to act more like a bouncer than a receptionist. His voice was like deep velvet, though, when he answered the phone. "Street Legal, how may I help you?"

Would he help her if she asked? Not if she needed help with Simon Kramer. Miguel was fiercely loyal to the managing partner of Street Legal. But she wouldn't need help. Simon wasn't going to attack her. Even if what had happened Friday night hadn't been a dream, he hadn't attacked.

He had seduced, which was far more dangerous. An attack she could have fought off. Even before moving to New York City six years ago, she had taken self-defense classes. She also carried Mace in her purse. She was prepared for an attack. She was not prepared for Simon Kramer's charm.

She couldn't believe she'd managed to walk away from him Friday night, that she hadn't been tempted to stay and find out if he was as good as all his ex-lovers had claimed. If he was the best...

She shivered and shook her head. No. He didn't tempt her. Not at all.

Liar, she called herself like he had called her that night.

The minute she stepped into her office, he turned

that charm on her, grinning at her from where he re-
clined in her chair, his feet up on her desk. That grin
stole away the breath she'd drawn. He was so damn
good-looking. The grin didn't just curve his sensual
lips and show his perfectly straight white teeth; it
made his blue eyes sparkle, highlighting the glint
of mischief in them.

As if she'd looked directly at the sun, she squeezed
her eyes shut for a moment. But when she opened
them again, he was still there. Ignoring her pounding
pulse and heart, she narrowed her eyes and focused
on him. Sure, his masculine beauty would probably
burn her retinas, but she risked it to study him. Despite the grin and the relaxed posture, he had tension
in his broad shoulders and the rigid line of his jaw.

Something was bothering him. She doubted he
was that upset about her resignation. Sure, hiring a
new assistant would be an inconvenience, but he'd
barely noticed let alone appreciated her these past
two years.

His grin widened, and he greeted her with a
"Good morning, sunshine."

The greeting was more apt for him. With his
golden-blond hair and sparkling smile, he was the
sun. With her dark hair and eyes, she felt more like
a dark cloud, especially after her sleepless nights
since Friday. How could she have just dreamed that
kiss when she hadn't slept at all?

And from the way he was looking at her, his gaze
moving like a caress up and down her body, she

knew it had happened. He hadn't just kissed her, though. He'd touched her.

Even though he hadn't moved from her chair, she felt his touch again. Felt his fingertips gliding over her skin...

And another shiver chased down her spine, making her skin tingle.

His grin widened.

She glared at him. "Apparently, you've already filled my position," she said. "So it's not necessary for me to work out my notice."

He laughed now, a deep chuckle that affected her nearly as much as his kiss and his touch had. It was so damn sexy. Just like he was.

She turned on the pointy heel of her pump and headed toward the door of her office. Her space was so much smaller than his, with just a few feet between her desk and the door. But she didn't make it before a strong hand closed around her arm and jerked her to a halt.

"You're not going anywhere," he told her.

She tugged, but his fingers were locked around her arm, his grasp too strong for her to break. Even though she wore one of her long-sleeved cardigans, she could feel the warmth of his skin through the fabric, and goose bumps of awareness rose on her skin.

"I am leaving," she said.

"Not for two weeks." Using his hand on her arm, he spun her around as if they were on a dance floor.

But Bette was not graceful, especially in heels.

She stumbled and fell against him. Her breath escaped her lungs in a gasp as her breasts pressed against his chest. Her hips pressed against his, and she felt his reaction to her closeness.

Instead of being embarrassed or apologetic, he chuckled. "I fully intend to enjoy every minute of these two weeks," he told her as he pushed his hips more firmly against hers. "And I'll make sure you enjoy them, too."

Heat rushed through her from her nipples, which had tightened against the silk cups of her bra, down to her clit, which pulsed with desire for him. *Damn him...*

"If I'd enjoyed working for you, I wouldn't have given my notice," she said as she stepped back. She needed space between them. But with his hand on her arm, she could only get inches and couldn't escape the heat of his body.

She needed feet. No, she needed miles. Miles between them would be good. Then she might not feel him, might not want him.

He lifted his free hand toward her face and ran his fingertips along her cheek. "That was because I wasn't making sure you enjoyed it," he said. He stepped closer and lowered his head. His lips were just a breath away from hers when he added, "You will enjoy working for me now, Bette. You'll enjoy it so much that you will never want to stop."

With the heat of his breath against her lips, she

could smell a trace of mint and coffee and could almost taste him. Not the mint and coffee but him…

How he'd tasted Friday night. Dark and rich and hot.

That desire pulsing in her core had Bette leaning toward him. She wanted his lips against hers again. She wanted to make sure that the kiss—*his kiss*—hadn't been a dream or, worse yet, just a manifestation of two years of longing. Longing for his kiss, his touch.

When her lips touched his, a jolt of sexual awareness shot so violently through her that she jerked back, fast and strongly enough that she pulled free of him. But it didn't matter that he was no longer touching her. He still had a hold on her—with his charm, with his aura.

And he knew it. The knowledge was in his grin and the sparkle in his blue eyes. She had no doubt he would use the power of that attraction over her.

For what? To convince her to stay?

She was not going to change her mind. Street Legal was never where she'd wanted to be. Law was not her passion. And Simon Kramer would not sway her with his charm and his good looks.

"Oh, Bette," he murmured with an ever-widening grin, "you and I are finally going to have some fun."

Fun? That she doubted, just like she'd doubted her earlier pep talk to herself.

Two weeks wasn't nothing. If he kept turning on the charm like this, it would be a lifetime. And because of that damn employment contract he'd had her sign, she wouldn't be able to cut that time. But he could. He was the only one who could waive the requirement for her to work out the two-week notice.

What would it take for him to get rid of her right away? Then she remembered what he'd asked her Friday night when he'd caught her leaving the resignation letter on his desk—the reason he'd thought she was leaving. That she was in love with him...

What if she hadn't laughed? What if she'd answered yes? Would he have shown her the door right then and taken away her key? Was that why she'd sent flowers to so many women for him over the past two years?

Because they'd fallen in love with him and had gotten clingy and desperate and he'd wanted nothing to do with them? From their calls pleading with her to let them talk to him, to see him...just one more time.

Yes. She knew what it would take to make him want to get rid of her right away. She would have to convince him that she'd fallen for him.

CHAPTER THREE

Simon did not miss the sudden sparkle in her eyes
and the slight curve of her lips. Bette Monroe was up
to something. And he had a feeling he wasn't going
to like it. It wouldn't be the first thing she'd done
that he didn't like. He didn't like her giving notice.
If she was the mole, he sure as hell didn't like that
she'd sold secrets from their case files. And if she
was the mole, he would make damn certain she paid
dearly for her betrayal.

As if she'd read his mind, her smile slid away, the
brightness of her dark eyes dimmed and she shivered.
She couldn't be cold, not with another damn sweater
buttoned up to her neck like it was. What was she
wearing beneath that? More lace and silk like on Friday night? Or had she only worn that because she'd
been meeting someone after she'd left him?

He wanted to find out what she was wearing beneath
her conservative skirt and sweater. He fully intended
to find out. But he'd have to be patient for now as the
phone on her desk began to ring.

A shaky sigh slipped through her lips as if she was

relieved for the interruption, and she reached for the phone. But before she could pick it up, he caught her wrist in his hand.

"Before you answer that," he said, "we need to go over our schedule for the day." He stroked his thumb over the silky skin of her delicate wrist, and her pulse leaped beneath his touch. "And the night."

Her throat moved as if she had to swallow before asking, "Night?"

He grinned. "Yes, we're going to be working late."

"H-how late?" she stammered.

"Quite late," he warned her. "Tonight and every night for the next two weeks. At least…"

She drew in a shaky breath now. "Two weeks," she said. "Just two weeks." And she reached for the phone with her other hand, lifting it to her flushed face.

"Bette Monroe, assistant to Simon Kramer, how may I help you?" she asked the caller.

She could tell Simon the damn truth. But he didn't expect her to freely divulge her secrets. Few people were honest about everything, and some, like his old man, were never honest about anything. He wasn't certain into which category Bette Monroe would fall. But just like he intended to find out what lingerie— if any—she was wearing, he fully intended to find that out, too.

He would execute the plan he'd concocted Friday night and seduce the truth out of his sexy executive assistant. He just hadn't realized how damn much he was going to enjoy the seduction. For the first time in a long time, he might actually have found a challenge. Ironically enough, it—*she*—had been right under his nose for the past two years.

While he had noticed Bette's ass and hips and the swell of her breasts beneath those sweaters, he'd never thought she could possibly be nearly as big a con as he was. He'd have to be careful that she didn't get access to any more case files and that she didn't get to him any more than she had already started to.

Just that faint brush of her lips across his had his pulse leaping like hers did beneath the pressure of his thumb. Just seeing her had his dick swelling behind the fly of his suit pants.

Damn. He wanted her. Seducing the truth out of her wouldn't be a hardship for him. Well, especially once he got a release from the tension building inside him.

He watched her lips move as she spoke to whoever had called. The dimple in the full bottom one seemed to wink at him, tempting him to take her mouth again—to kiss her like he had Friday night. It had been one damn long weekend waiting for Monday, waiting to see her again, to touch her again, to kiss her...

But she had work to do. And so did he. He had to plan his next move in the seduction of his sexy little office mole.

Just one week and four days left...

That was what Bette told herself as lights began to shut off on the floor for the Street Legal law practice.

Miguel had left for the night along with most of the rest of the office staff. Actually, she wasn't certain if there was anyone else on the floor but her.

Simon hadn't lied about working late. Fortunately, working was pretty much all he'd been doing—meeting with clients in and out of the office throughout the day. Of course every time he'd had a free minute, he had either stopped by her desk or called her into his office. And every time, he had treated her to another strong dose of his sexiness until she'd gotten drunk on it.

Maybe that was why she felt so light-headed now. Or maybe it was because she'd been so busy herself that she'd had to skip lunch. She would not survive nine more days like today, not with her sanity intact. She had to make him cut the two weeks short.

Very short.

Like she wished this day would have been. Would it ever end? Simon had left a while ago for his last appointment, but he'd given her orders—with a wink and a grin—for her to stay until he returned. And the way he'd looked at her...like he was already undressing her.

Her face had flushed and her body had heated and she'd tried to stammer out a protest. But he'd only laughed and claimed he would have notes for her that wouldn't wait until morning. He was enjoying this...enjoying how rattled she got when he turned his notorious charm on her.

She could not let it affect her anymore. In order to get him to cut short the two weeks, she would have to rattle him instead. And she knew just how to do that—act like she was in love with him.

She didn't have any experience in the theater, though. Unlike so many other women, she hadn't come to New York to be an actress. She had come to be a fashion designer. But apparently, she had acted her ass off the past two years as an executive assistant in a law firm.

She could do this. She *had* to do this.

The elevator dinged. Here was her curtain call.

She drew in a deep breath and forced a bright smile. But she didn't hear the quick taps of Simon's shoes against the hardwood floor. Instead, she heard the creak and whine of metal wheels rolling over the wood.

"What the hell...?" she murmured. And she stood to peer into the reception area just as a chef, complete with tall hat, white uniform and apron, rolled in the metal cart she'd heard.

He paused in her doorway. "You—Miss Monroe?" he asked, his accent thick and impossible to place—at least for Bette.

Despite six years of living in the melting pot of New York City, the only accents she could readily place were ones like her own: Midwestern. This man could have been French, Belgian, Swiss, Austrian or faking it. There were a lot of people in this city who pretended to be from someplace they were not. Who pretended to be what they were not.

So she should be able to pretend with Simon.

This man she answered honestly, "Yes, I'm Bette Monroe."

The chef's beady-eyed gaze traveled from her hair, drawn into that tight bun, down to the closed toes of her pumps and back. His brow furrowed as if he doubted her. Would she have to show her license?

She hoped not because whatever he had on that cart, simmering in chafing dishes with burners beneath them, smelled like heaven—if heaven smelled like savory spices and beef and potatoes.

Her stomach growled, and her mouth began to water.

The guy made a noise, too, in his throat. It was either a groan of disgust or exasperation. "Mr. Kramer said you would be expecting me."

She glanced at her computer, which was open to her email, then down at her phone, which had no new texts. "Mr. Kramer didn't mention you to me yet."

What was this? Along with the chafing dishes were two plates, cloth napkins and a couple of candles ready to light. A romantic dinner for two? Who was Simon meeting here?

The elevator dinged again and she realized she was about to find out. But the taps were Simon's quick footsteps, not the clicks of a woman's heels. At least he had arrived before his date.

"Bruno!" Simon exclaimed as he strode through the reception area and saw the chef standing just outside the open door to Bette's office. "Excellent timing."

"She did not know I was coming," Bruno remarked as if disparaging Bette for not being psychic. He was definitely not criticizing Simon for not telling her. From the way he stared at Simon, it was clear he found nothing wrong with the blond lawyer and everything right.

Simon grinned. "Of course not. It's a surprise."

"For me?" Bette asked as her heart began to thump faster and harder.

"There is no one else," Simon said with a wink.

She bit her bottom lip to hold in the laugh at the blatant lie. She'd never known him to date only one woman at a time—if what he did could actually be called dating.

More like heart breaking...

Her heart rate quickened with the reminder. But now, with his gaze turned on her, she understood how he'd broken so many hearts. He wasn't just outrageously good-looking, as if that wasn't enough.

"Bruno, please set up in my office." Simon directed him, gesturing with his briefcase toward his closed door.

Bruno nodded and wheeled his cart away. And Bette's stomach growled in protest.

Simon raised a golden-blond brow. "Sounds like Bruno arrived just in time."

Heat rushed toward her face. "I skipped lunch," she explained.

"I know," Simon said. "Miguel told me. That's why I asked Bruno to prepare dinner for us."

She shook her head. "That's not necessary. I can eat when I get home." And work. She had so much to do for her new job. She really needed to cut short these two weeks—as short as she possibly could.

"That won't be for a while yet," he told her.

"But—but it's already so late…" From last Friday night, she knew that it was not a good idea to be alone in the office with him.

"We will work over dinner," he said, "and finish up so you can get home to your…" He raised an eyebrow again as he waited for her reply.

"Apartment."

It wasn't any of his business why she was quitting; it wasn't any of his business if she lived with someone or had a boyfriend. The less Simon Kramer knew about her the better off she would be.

He was undeterred and asked, "Is anyone waiting for you in that apartment?"

She let a smile slip out as she shook her head. "No. I don't have a cat. And the building doesn't allow dogs."

"Good," he said. "I'm allergic."

She wanted to tell him that there was no way in hell he was ever coming to her apartment. But before the words slipped out like her smile had, she remembered her plan. So she smiled wider and murmured, "Then it's good I don't have one."

His blue eyes momentarily widened with surprise at her remark before narrowing with obvious suspicion. He studied her face. "So you're going to invite me to your place?"

Her pulse kicked into overdrive, racing away. She was nervous about her plan. She wasn't imagining him in her apartment, although he would look damn good in her new place. That wasn't going to happen. Ever.

"That wouldn't be appropriate while I'm still working for you," she said. Then, summoning all the acting ability she possessed, she batted her lashes at him. "Guess you'll have to wait two weeks for that invitation."

He laughed and shook his head. "I've never been a patient man, Bette."

Bette had more ability to be patient than act. She'd had to wait to move away from her small hometown in Michigan to attend fashion school and move to New York. She'd also had to wait six years for the career she'd wanted, for which she'd worked so hard, to finally take off. But now that it had, her patience had worn thin. There was no way she was waiting two weeks to end her relationship with Simon Kramer, such that it was.

"I can leave now," she offered. "A temp service could send over someone until you hire my replacement."

He laughed again and reached for her arm, tugging her toward him. "Oh, Bette, think of all the fun you'd miss if you left so soon."

"Fun?" she parroted. "I thought we were working over dinner."

He stepped closer, so that his body brushed against hers, his thigh touching hers, his chest bumping hers as he breathed deeply. Then he leaned down and murmured, "Work is very fun for me."

She knew that was true. He obviously loved being a lawyer, probably loved being the managing partner of Street Legal even more. What she couldn't understand was his sudden interest in her. Was it only because she was leaving?

Something about wanting what you couldn't have?

She hoped that was the case, so that when she made it clear he could have her, he wouldn't want her. Instead of stepping back as she had every time before, she stepped closer to him, pressing her body even tighter against his. She felt his erection pushing against her hip. And she parted her lips with a gasp. He felt big—really big—rubbing against her.

His gaze dropped to her mouth. His pupils dilated until they swallowed the bright blue. And he lowered his head even closer to hers.

"Dinner is served," Bruno called out, his accent not nearly as thick now, from Simon's office.

Her boss groaned and released a shuddery sigh. "We'll eat first," he said.

First?

What else did he have planned besides work and dinner? Bette's knees trembled a bit as she walked with him the short distance to his office. As if she didn't know where it was, he moved his hand to the small of her back, guiding her. Or branding her?

She felt the heat of his palm through her sweater and the lace camisole she wore beneath it over her bra. His hand was big, so big that his fingers reached over the top curve of her butt. Could he feel the bow at the top of the G-string she wore beneath her pencil-slim skirt? A matching bow held together the cups of her bra.

She always wore lingerie—for a few reasons. He was not one of them. But would he think she'd worn it for him—if she dared show it to him?

The heat already flushing her body increased, burning her up. The lack of food and all the doses of his charm must have addled her brain. She wasn't thinking clearly at all, not like she'd been when she'd turned in her resignation. Then she'd been thinking more clearly than she had in the two years she'd worked for him.

His fingers moved, sliding over that bow, as if he was trying to figure out what it was. He glanced down at her, and again his eyes had widened with a look of surprise. "How is it, Bette, that we've worked together for two years but yet I don't feel as if I know you at all?"

She could have told him that she'd just been lucky all these years to have escaped his notice. She had been just an office fixture to him, like a computer or the coffeepot. But she only smiled and shook her head. "I have no idea."

"Well, let's fix that," he said. And finally, albeit reluctantly, he removed his hand from her ass and held out a chair for her. His office was so large that in addition to his desk and chair, he had a couch and a small conference room table and chairs.

Bruno had set up their feast, complete with lit candles, on that table. The tall windows looking out over Midtown reflected back the flickering flames. She smiled at the chef as she took her seat, but his only interest was in Simon. She was surprised that he wasn't holding out his chair.

"Is everything to your satisfaction?" the chef asked as he poured glasses of wine.

Simon took the chair right next to her and picked up the wineglass. He swirled the red liquid, studied the glass as the wine slid down the sides of it, then he sniffed it, all before taking a sip.

Bette usually went out with guys who drank beer or mixed cocktails. The few wine drinkers she'd dated had performed the same ritual Simon had but with them it had seemed pretentious and unnecessary. Simon seemed to know what he was doing and why.

She had no doubts—from the calls of all those desperate women—that he was the same with sex. That he knew what he was doing and why.

She drew in a shaky breath.

Finally, he took a sip. But he held it in his mouth for several moments before swallowing. "Excellent," he said. Then he held out a glass to her.

She usually drank white wine. Reds were too bitter for her taste. But she was too intrigued to find out what he considered excellent to refuse the glass. Like him, she took only a sip and held it in her mouth for several seconds. Flavor burst on her tongue. She could taste berries and spices; it was as rich and full of nuances as his kiss had been, as he was.

She let it slide down her throat, enjoying the sensation and the taste. "Excellent," she agreed.

Bruno lifted the lids from their plates. "And the meal, Mr. Kramer?"

Beef Wellington with steamed vegetables and parsnips and red-skin potatoes. Bette's mouth watered, reminding her of how hungry she was—for food. Ever since Simon had come back to the office, she'd been hungry for something else.

For more of his kisses, more of his touch.

More of his lethal charm.

As Simon cut through the flaky pastry and the meat, juices oozed onto the plate, swirling around the potatoes and vegetables. Like with the wine, he took just a small bite and held it in his mouth for a long moment before chewing and swallowing. Then he sighed and pronounced it excellent, as well.

Bette's heart pounded in anticipation and not just of the meal. Would sex be the same way with Simon? Would he savor every moment of it?

He cut another bite and held it out to her. Again she copied him, closing her lips around it before holding it on her tongue. The spices and flavor of the meat overwhelmed her with pleasure. She chewed and swallowed, and a moan of that pleasure slipped through her lips.

Simon groaned. Then he glanced up at Bruno, as if just realizing the chef was still in the room with them. "You can go," he said. "I'll have Miguel return everything to you in the morning."

Bruno hesitated, but then, obviously realizing arguing with a lawyer would not be smart, he nodded and left, closing the door behind him.

Once again, Bette was alone with Simon Kramer. Her fingers trembled as she reached for her glass of wine. She was afraid and not just of what he would do. She was afraid of what she would have to do in order to carry out her plan. How the hell could she convince him that she was falling for him and that if she did, she would get clingy and crazy?

She'd been so focused on her designs and her career that she'd never really fallen for anyone before. Unlike her mom and sister, she hadn't been about to let any man mess with her plans. So she had no idea how to act in love, especially with someone like Simon Kramer for whom she would never be stupid enough to fall.

For the past two years she'd seen exactly how he treated women—like they were disposable. And to him, they were. Even before he'd dumped one, another had come along. But that was a good thing for her.

He always dumped them.

So if she could pretend to fall for him, he would

dump her, as well. But how far would she have to go to convince him she was falling?

Just being alone with him was a risk. Not that he would ever physically hurt her. He didn't have to physically coerce anyone to do his bidding. He used his sex appeal instead.

And even though she knew exactly what he was doing and that it was just a game to him, she was not immune.

She doubted she would escape this time with just a kiss. But she wasn't entirely sure that she would mind. For two years she'd dreamed of what it would be like to have his attention turned on her. For two years she'd imagined how his kiss would taste, how his touch would feel.

Now she knew. And she wanted more.

CHAPTER FOUR

For the past two years Simon had surreptitiously ogled his assistant, but he'd had no idea that she might wear lingerie beneath those tight skirts and buttoned-up cardigans of hers even though he had seen lace peek out between those buttons. Friday night he'd seen that lace when he'd undone a few of those buttons and discovered that sexy bustier. He wanted to undo all the buttons tonight, and he wanted to unzip that skirt and peel it off her luscious ass.

He wanted Bette Monroe.

His hand shaking a little, he set his wineglass back on the table. He hadn't had much to drink but he made a point to never overindulge. At least not on alcohol...

He wanted nothing affecting his mind or his control. But Bette, sitting close to him, was affecting the hell out of him. What was wrong with him? When he was focused on something—like he was now on finding the office mole—he was never distracted from his task.

But she distracted him. He watched her lips part as she forked in a bite of steamed broccoli, and he wished her lips were parting for his tongue. While Bruno's food was as incredible as it always was, Simon wanted to taste her more than the meal.

And not just her lips or her mouth.

"What?" she asked as she lifted her hand to her face. "Do I have broccoli in my teeth?"

He shook his head.

"Why are you staring at me?" she asked.

She really didn't seem to know. He wasn't used to that, not when he usually dated models and actresses whose egos rivaled his.

"Are you completely unaware of how beautiful you are?" he asked.

Her lips curved into a smile but it was a little mocking and she murmured, "For the past two years, you were *completely* unaware of me."

He grinned. "That's what you thought?"

"It's what I know," she said. "I might as well have been a copy machine for all the attention you paid me the past two years."

He narrowed his eyes and studied her face. Was that why she'd done it, why she'd given information to the opposition? Because she'd been resentful that he had never seemed to notice her?

"Did you want my attention?" he asked.

Her gaze slipped away from his, and her teeth nipped into her bottom lip. Maybe she was too embarrassed to admit that she'd wanted him to notice her, so he assured her, "You had my attention."

Her teeth still nibbling on that full, sexy lower lip, she shook her head. "I find that very hard to believe."

His seduction wouldn't work if she didn't believe that he found her attractive. So he leaned closer, pressing his thigh against hers, and he murmured, "I have spent countless hours admiring your ass...ets."

Her lips curved into a smile. "If only that were true." She gave a wistful sigh then.

"You really did want me to notice you?" he asked as a warning bell began to sound inside his head. She was acting very differently than she had Friday night when she'd left her resignation on his desk.

Her brown eyes widened behind the lenses of her glasses, and her lashes fluttered. "Yes..." Then she leaned against him, and her fingertips skimmed over his thigh.

His body tensed, with her touch and with the thought that just dawned on him. Maybe he wasn't the only one turning on the charm. He had a feeling he was definitely getting played.

For what? More case file secrets?

But he was curious as to how far she would carry her charade. So he covered her hand with his and guided her fingers to stroke up and down his thigh.

She glanced sideways at him, and her lips curved into a smile while her already-dark eyes darkened more with desire. Or was that wishful thinking on his part? Then she moved her hand farther up his leg, toward his groin.

And he sucked in a sharp breath. "Bette..."

She tugged her hand from beneath his and brought it back to the stem of her wineglass. Then she stroked her fingers up and down it, like he wanted them stroking up and down his cock. Mischief sparkled in her dark eyes; she was completely aware of what he wanted, what he needed.

The need startled him. Sure, he'd felt desire before. Often. As a teen runaway, he'd wanted so much stuff—stuff he hadn't had. Like a safe place to sleep, food, clothes.

He'd wanted those things so badly that he'd used some questionable methods to get them. But he'd succeeded then, just as he would now. He would succeed in getting the truth out of Bette.

The truth wasn't all he wanted from her. He wanted release from the tension gripping his body. He was so damn tense that when she leaned against him, he jumped a little, making his chair squeak and nearly tip.

Her smile widened. And he knew for certain he was being played. While he hadn't been as unaware of her as she'd thought these past two years, he'd had no idea what she was really like—or who she really was.

But he intended to find out. He had to regain control in order to do that, though—over himself and over her. So he reached around her and poured some more wine in her glass.

She giggled and asked, "Are you trying to get me drunk to have your way with me?"

"Would it work?" he wondered aloud.

"I'm a lightweight," she said. "Just a few more sips and I'll either be stripping off my clothes or passing out." She brought the rim to her lips and tipped up the glass for a long, deep sip.

"If I have a vote in this, I'd prefer the stripping," he teased.

She arched a dark brow above the top frame of her glasses and murmured, "I'm sure you would."

Was she mocking him? The arched-brow gesture was one he'd been doing since he was a kid. While he wasn't as aware of her as he obviously should have been the past two years, she seemed to have been aware of him.

"Do you play cards?" he asked.

"Why are you asking?"

"I was thinking we could play a hand or two of poker—strip poker." He was really good at cards but most especially at poker.

She giggled again. "We're supposed to be working," she reminded him. "Not playing. You said this was a working dinner, something about taking notes."

He chuckled now. "Oh, I'm taking notes."

But he hadn't learned much about her yet.

"I'm supposed to be taking notes," she said.

He touched the stem of her glass as she took another sip. "You're too drunk." Was she? He wanted her, but he didn't want to take advantage of her.

"Nope," she said. "I'm just drunk enough." And she rose from the chair.

Maybe she meant that she was sober enough, to know to leave before he seduced her, like he'd intended. Disappointment gripped him. He wouldn't try too hard to persuade her to stay, not if she'd truly had too much to drink.

He narrowed his eyes. "Just drunk enough for what?"

She pulled her glasses off her nose and dropped them onto the table next to her barely touched meal. Bruno would be so disappointed that they hadn't eaten much.

But Simon wasn't hungry for food. And despite her stomach growling earlier, Bette hadn't eaten very much. That was probably why the wine had hit her so hard—hard enough—that she reached up and tugged the pins from her hair. The sable-brown tresses tumbled down, falling in thick waves nearly to her waist.

He groaned. She was so damn sexy.

Then she reached for the buttons on her cardigan. She flicked open the first one and the second one. And Simon jumped to his feet and stepped close to her. Like he had when she'd touched his leg, he covered her hand with his. But now he stopped her fingers from moving.

"You're not drunk enough," he corrected her. "You're too drunk."

She tilted her head and stared up at him as if surprised. "You really want me to stop?"

"Hell, no," he admitted. "I want you to undo every one of those damn buttons. I want you to unzip your skirt and take off your clothes, so I can see what the hell you're wearing underneath them." Because it was driving him crazy imagining her in lace and nothing else.

She stepped back and pulled her hand free of his. Then she continued undoing her buttons until the cardigan parted and slid down her arms. She wore a lace camisole that was so thin he could see the bra beneath it.

"Bette," he murmured, but he couldn't summon the protest he knew he should be making.

She touched her hip, pulling down the tab of the zipper until her wool skirt dropped to her feet.

His breath escaped in a gasp.

Her underwear was lace, too—black like the camisole and the bra beneath it. Then she tugged the camisole up and over her head until it fell to the floor atop the skirt.

"Damn," he cursed her. She tested his control in a way it had never been tested before. He closed his eyes, but he couldn't shut out the image of her standing before him in that sexy black underwear. Her breasts nearly overflowed the cups of that black bra, and those cups were held together with only a bow.

He had to know. So he opened his eyes again, and he spun her around. Just as he'd suspected, there was a bow at the top of her luscious ass holding together the lace panel at the front of her panties to the tiny panel in the back.

And the control he'd fought so hard to regain snapped completely. He'd intended to seduce her, but she was the one seducing him. "Bette, what the hell are you doing?"

Bette couldn't answer his question because she had no idea what the hell she was doing, either. Despite what she'd said, that she was just drunk enough, she would be able to remember with perfect clarity what she'd just done, how she'd just undressed for him...

And worse yet, he wasn't drunk at all, so he would remember, as well. He stepped closer to her, and his hands gripped her shoulders. "What the hell are you doing?" he asked again, his voice gruff while his eyes were completely black. The pupils had swallowed his blue irises whole.

"I'm a horrible poker player," she said. "So I just saved myself the trouble."

"I didn't think you wanted to play."

She was playing a very dangerous game. She wanted Simon Kramer to think she was in love with him, so that he'd cut short her two-week notice. She didn't want to actually fall for him.

Of course she was in no danger of that. She knew him far better than he knew her. No woman ever held his interest for very long. Since he hadn't even noticed her the past two years, she was surprised she had his interest right now.

Maybe that was because of the underwear...

He stared at the bow between the cups of her bra. And she smiled as pride surged through her. The pride was in the design, though. And maybe in the fact that she knew she had his attention now.

His full attention.

"I never said I didn't want to play," she reminded him. "I just thought we were supposed to be working."

"It's working," he said, his hands sliding from her shoulders down her bare arms. "Whatever game you're playing is working."

She widened her eyes and feigned innocence. "What game? I told you I'm no good at poker."

He narrowed his eyes and studied her face. "Oh, I think you're a damn good poker player, Bette Monroe."

She reached for his tie and tugged the knot loose. "Then you better take off your clothes, too..." She moved her fingers to the buttons on his shirt, undoing them like she'd undone her cardigan. "Since you're losing."

"I am losing," Simon said, his chest rising and falling with his erratic breathing. "You've completely taken control."

She smiled again at the frustration and desire she heard in his voice. Her fingers skimmed down his washboard abs to the buckle of his belt.

"No," he said, and his hand caught hers. "You don't understand."

"What?" she asked. "What don't I understand?"

"*I* don't lose control," he told her.

She smiled but assured him, "You haven't." He hadn't even touched her. Maybe the underwear wasn't as sexy as she'd thought it was, as it made her feel.

"If you're just playing some game with me, you better stop," he told her. "Because I really—genuinely—want you." For two years she'd wondered what it would feel like to have him look at her the way she looked at him, with appreciation and attraction. He was so damn handsome that he was actually beautiful. Beautifully masculine. Muscles rippled beneath her touch as she tugged her hands from his and skimmed her palms up his chest to push his shirt and suitcoat from his broad shoulders. Muscles rippled in his arms, too, when he shrugged it off.

For two years she'd dreamed about him turning his attention to her, about him seducing her as he'd seduced so many other women into losing their minds and hearts to him. She knew he didn't want either her mind or her heart, though. So they would be quite safe from him. He wanted only her body. And she wanted his.

She had been so busy lately that she hadn't had any time to date. It had been a while for her since she'd had sex with anything not battery-operated. And it had never been Simon. She wanted to experience his notorious sexual prowess while she had the opportunity. And she didn't have to worry about losing her job afterward. She actually hoped that she did.

"I don't want you to stop," she assured him.

"Good," he said. That control he'd sounded so worried about must have snapped because he dragged her against his hard, tense body and lowered his mouth to hers.

He kissed her as if he was starving, nibbling and nipping at her lips. She gasped as his teeth tugged on her lower lip. Then his tongue slid inside her mouth, mating with hers.

Her pulse pounded while heat rushed through her body. She didn't feel the least bit of chill, standing in his loftlike office in only her thin lace lingerie, especially as his hands began to move over her body. His touch spread fire through her.

Tension wound tightly inside her core. She needed the release that she instinctively knew he could give her. But he seemed to be in no hurry to do anything but kiss her.

And a kiss had never turned her on as much. He stroked his tongue in and out of her mouth like she wanted his cock sliding in and out of her body. She moaned.

And he groaned in response. "You taste so damn good…" he murmured against her lips.

"It's the wine…"

"It's you…" Finally, he lifted his head from hers. But he stepped back.

She thought maybe he'd changed his mind; maybe he didn't really want her. But his chest rose and fell with pants for breath, and she understood that he was just fighting again, fighting hard to regain control of himself.

She wanted him out of control. So she lifted her fingers to the bow between her breasts.

But he caught her hand and pulled it away. Then he shook his head. "No…"

She stared up at him through her lashes and asked, "You don't want me?"

He groaned again. "I want you too damn much." And he didn't sound happy about it. "So let me do this…" He tugged on the bow until it slipped free of its knot, and the cups of the bra parted, falling away from her breasts. The bra dropped to the hardwood floor atop her clothes.

He cursed. And his skin flushed like hers, with passion. "Damn, Bette…"

She wasn't cold, so that wasn't why her nipples tightened. It was desire. For him.

He touched her. His fingers sliding from where he'd untied the bow between her breasts up to her collarbone and her neck. He found her pulse and traced his fingertip over it. It leaped like her desire for him.

And he must have known it. He smiled, just slightly, as if it was all he could manage with his lips parted as he panted for breath. His chest—his glorious naked chest—rose and fell, muscles rippling.

She had to touch, too. So she slid her hands over his skin. Soft, golden hair tickled her palms. How could he look like an angel but be such a devil—in business and pleasure?

She didn't care, though. She wouldn't be working for him much longer. And she was never really going to fall for him. But she had to convince him that she might. So she said, "I've wanted you for so long."

His eyes narrowed slightly as if he doubted her. But then he must have remembered how handsome he was because he nodded in acceptance.

And she smiled.

"You're not drunk enough," he murmured. But he didn't reach for the wine to pour her any more. Instead he reached for her. "You're too in control," he said, as if it was a complaint.

Then he proceeded to drive her out of her mind with his touch. His hands moved over her breasts, gently kneading and stroking while his palms brushed over and over her already tight nipples.

She moaned and leaned toward him, needing more.

He gave more. His hands moved down to her hips, and he tugged at the bows holding her panties in place. They fell onto her bra and clothes. Bette might have fallen, too, as her knees began to shake, but he lifted her into his arms. Her breasts rubbed against his naked chest as he carried her across the office to his couch.

The leather was cold against her back and butt and thighs, but it did nothing to cool the heat of her passion-flushed skin. She locked her arms around his neck, trying to pull him down with her. But he held back and knelt beside the couch. Then he feasted on her body as if she were a banquet Bruno had laid out for his pleasure.

But the pleasure was all hers.

He kissed her lips—just briefly, nibbling gently at them. Then her chin before he moved his mouth to her breasts. As he kissed them, his hands moved lower, over the curve of her hip and down the length of her thighs.

She shivered as sensations raced through her.

He pulled back. "Are you cold?"

Too choked with desire to speak, she shook her head.

He smiled now. He was back in control. Not just of himself but of her. And he knew it.

Before she could protest, though, he moved his mouth back to her breast and closed his lips over a nipple. As he tugged at it, she felt heat and moisture rush straight to her core. Then his hand was there, his fingers moving inside her. She arched against his hand, and he rubbed his palm against her mound.

"Simon…" His name slipped out on a gasp of pleasure.

"Bette," he murmured. "You're so damn hot!"

And whatever control he'd regained snapped. "I have to taste you." And his mouth replaced his hand between her legs. He dipped his tongue inside her, teasing her and building the tension. Then he withdrew it and flicked it over her clit.

She rose up and cried out as an orgasm shot through her.

He groaned. "You are so damn responsive..." But he stood up and moved away from her.

She reached out in protest. The orgasm had been good, better than she achieved on her own. But she knew there was more. She held out her arms to him.

But he stepped back and stared down at her. And disappointment filled her that he might stop. He unclasped his belt and pushed down his pants and briefs. He was so damn beautiful—his dick so long and hard as it jutted from a bed of curls even more golden than the hair on his head.

Somehow, as if he was a magician, a condom appeared in his hand. He tore the packet and rolled it over his cock. Then he joined her on the couch, connecting their bodies.

He stretched, then filled her. Bette arched and adjusted, making room for his impressive length and girth. She was so hot and wet that it was easy. And it felt right, like he fitted perfectly inside her.

He lifted her legs so that he sank even deeper and began to thrust in and out. Bette came again—that quickly—just from his movements. He was that damn good...

But then he got better. He leaned down and arched his back until his mouth could close over the point of one of her breasts. He sucked on the nipple as he moved.

Tension spiraled inside her again, and Bette arched and shifted, seeking to release it. She bucked beneath him, losing all control. They moved in a frenzy, like they were convulsing and then she did—as the orgasm slammed through her. Her muscles quivered and sensations gripped her. She had never felt anything as intense for as long. She just kept coming, the pleasure overwhelming in intensity and duration. She screamed his name.

Then he tensed and cried out as he found his release. Panting for breath, he leaned his forehead against hers. Staring into her eyes, he asked, "What the hell was that?"

She had no idea, either, beyond the most passionate sexual experience she'd ever had. And because it was, she was too stunned to remember her act. She said nothing as he slipped away from her, into the bathroom off his office. But she moved, dressing more quickly than they'd had sex.

She didn't care if he wanted her to stay any longer. She had to get away. She had to regroup. So she left his office and stopped in hers only long enough to grab her phone and purse. Then she ran for the elevator, jabbing her finger against the button.

While she waited for the car to arrive, she heard him call her name. But before he found her, the elevator dinged and the doors opened. She jumped inside and jabbed at the button to close the doors. When they finally closed, she leaned against the wall and began to shake.

What the hell had she done?

CHAPTER FIVE

EVEN THOUGH HE'D SHOWERED, Simon could smell her
on his skin. Or maybe her scent was in his office.
Or, worse yet, in his head, just like the image of her
standing before him in nothing but that scandalous
lingerie—the lacy bra and panties with those stra-
tegically placed little bows. Bows that his fingers
twitched to untie yet again.

"Simon!" a deep voice yelled as fingers snapped
in his face. "What the hell's going on?"

He blinked but the image of Bette lingered yet in
his mind. He forced himself to focus on the men sitting around the conference table in his office. The
partners met every Tuesday morning, their slow day,
to discuss Street Legal. He should have told them
to meet him somewhere else, though, because he
couldn't focus in here.

It smelled like Bette, and it smelled like the ves-
tiges of their dinner the night before, even though
the metal cart with the dishes and wine bottle had
been returned to Bruno's restaurant. Another cart

sat next to the table, this one with a carafe of coffee and an assortment of fruit, Danish and croissants.

"Yeah," Stone said, his brow furrowed with concern. Then he echoed Ronan's question, "What the hell's going on with you? You're completely out of it."

Simon shrugged. "Nothing's going on." Except that he'd lost control last night. And that was something that never happened to him. He was supposed to have seduced Bette Monroe but she'd seduced him instead.

"Who is this woman that had you tearing out of the bar last Friday?" Trevor asked. "The one who sexted you?"

"Ah, that's why he left in such a damn hurry," Ronan said. Then he snorted derisively at himself. "I should've known it was because of a woman. Is that why you're so distracted right now?"

Simon snorted this time. "Like a woman has ever distracted me before..."

The others laughed, like he'd wanted them to, but he was unable to join in. He'd just misled his friends, and he'd never done that before. A woman had distracted him last night. He'd completely forgotten why he'd wanted to seduce her—for information, for evidence—not for pleasure. At least not just for pleasure.

But hell, what he'd felt last night with Bette had gone beyond pleasure. He'd never felt anything like that.

He'd wanted her so badly that he'd acted like a teenager—with no finesse. He'd just had to have her.

Especially after he'd tasted her. She was sweeter than any pastry on that cart. And hotter than the coffee steaming in the mugs on the table. So damn hot...

She'd nearly burned him as he'd plunged his cock into her. The sensation had been incredible. She was so tight, so wet. She'd fitted him perfectly. Then when she'd come, her inner muscles had rippled and squeezed him. And he'd completely lost it. He couldn't remember the last time he'd come that long or that hard.

"So if it's not a woman," Trevor said, "what's bothering you?"

He shrugged, but the tension remained in his shoulders and neck and lower in his body, where his groin swelled with the need to experience that beyond-pleasure release again. "Just had a busy day yesterday. Back-to-back meetings with clients or potential clients all day." And at night...

He had Bette. Or did she have him?

"Yeah," Stone said. "You worked really late last night."

Simon glanced up, and across the table he met his friend's intense gaze. The knowledge was in Stone's dark gray eyes. He knew...

"You were here?" Simon asked uneasily. He'd thought everyone was gone and that he and Bette had been alone in the office last night. Obviously, he'd thought wrong.

"I have to make sure my defense is ready before the trial begins," Stone said. His gaze increased in intensity. "And I have to make sure none of my defense plan leaks to the prosecution."

"Hillary Bellows," Trevor murmured with a lustful sigh. "I wouldn't mind going toe-to-toe with her."

Stone glared at him. "Yeah, you're an idiot, then. She's a pain in the ass."

"Because she's good," Trev goaded him.

"I'm better," Stone said. And it wasn't just his ego talking. All his past victories against her proved it true. "I will win this case as long as there are no surprises like there were in Trev's trial." He was staring at Simon again.

He nodded. "There will not be any surprises. Nobody's going to get into our files again." He would keep Bette too busy with work and sex to sell any more secrets.

"So you got it handled?" Trev asked. "You found out who got their hands on that report from my case files?"

He wasn't ready yet to share his suspicions about Bette. First, he had no proof. Second, if his partners knew he suspected her, they would want him to toss her out of the office immediately. And he wasn't ready to let her go just yet.

At least not until he had proof…

Then he would.

She hadn't given him much of a choice last night.

She'd run off before he'd finished cleaning up. He'd come so much—because of her.

"I'm working on it," he said. His voice sounded gruff, so he had to clear it before continuing. "But now that we're aware of what happened, we're all more vigilant. Nobody's going to pull anything on us again."

Least of all Bette Monroe. She would not seduce him again. That was not going to happen.

He slapped his palms onto the tabletop so forcefully that he had coffee spilling over the rim of his mug. "Anything else we need to discuss this morning?" And he gave Stone a pointed look, so that he wouldn't bring up what he knew about the night before—about Simon's late night with Bette.

Ronan, who was always full of energy, jumped up from his chair. "No. We're good. I trust that you've got everything handled. It's not like we could actually have a mole in our office anyway, not with you doing all the hiring."

Heat rushed to his face now from where it had pooled in his groin with thoughts of Bette. How had she fooled him so completely? She was nothing like what he'd thought she was the past two years.

If he'd only known how damn hot she was...

How responsive. She'd come so easily and so many times. He was good. But he wasn't that good. He hadn't even given her his best effort because he'd lost control. That damn tension had wound up so tightly inside him that he'd snapped completely.

Trev stood up, as well. "I'm the one with back-to-back appointments with potential clients all day today," he said and sighed. "The burden of being a winner. Everybody wants you."

Simon wriggled his eyebrows and grinned. "Everybody's always wanted me."

Apparently, even Bette...

But she'd never given him that impression before. Did she know that he was onto her? The thought of her distracted him again, so that he barely noticed that Ronan and Trevor had left his office.

Stone had remained, though, sitting across from him, his eyes narrowed as he studied Simon's face. "What the hell are you thinking?"

"Right now?" Simon asked. "I'm not sure you'd want to know." Unless Stone had a thing for Bette Monroe, too, because Simon couldn't stop thinking about her and that damn lacy lingerie she'd been wearing the night before. What would she be wearing today? He couldn't wait to find out.

"Last night," Stone said. "What the hell were you thinking?"

"What are you talking about?" Simon asked. He could probably guess, but he'd learned it was smarter not to make any assumptions. Maybe Stone didn't know who'd been in the office with Simon.

"I was here," Stone reminded him. "I heard Bruno wheel in the cart for your romantic dinner." His brow furrowed with either confusion or concern. "With your assistant."

Simon chuckled. "So—we were working late."

"You weren't working," Stone said. "Your office isn't soundproof and that wasn't dictation I overheard as I was leaving."

Heat rushed to Simon's face, but he chuckled again and teased, "Jealous?"

Stone shook his head. "Concerned that you're exposing Street Legal to a potential lawsuit. She's an employee."

"Not for much longer," Simon admitted.

Stone groaned. "You're firing her? That makes it even worse."

"No," Simon said. "She already gave her notice."

"Oh..." Stone nodded as if he suddenly understood.

But what could he understand? Simon hadn't told him that Bette could potentially be the mole. Again, he hesitated about revealing that information. It was smarter to keep his suspicions to himself until he had proof.

And yet he was compelled to ask his friend, "What does that mean?"

"I've seen the way you looked at her the past couple of years," Stone said. "So I get you going all out since she's no longer off-limits."

Hell, if she was the mole, she'd be more off-limits than she was as an active employee.

"All out?"

"The fancy dinner, the seduction..."

He was responsible for the fancy dinner, but the

seduction had been more her than him. He shrugged. "What can I say?"

Stone sighed. "I just hope you know what you're doing," he murmured as he stood up and headed toward the door.

Simon got up and followed him out. He hoped he knew what the hell he was doing, too. The first thing he did was head to Bette's office. But it was dark and empty. As he turned around in the doorway, Miguel waved him over to the reception desk in the lobby and informed him. "She called in sick."

Yeah, right...

She wasn't sick. She was scared, scared that he was going to find out what she was up to. And she was damn right to be scared because he was more determined than ever to get the truth out of Bette Monroe.

Unfortunately—after last night—that wasn't all he wanted from her.

Bette twirled in front of the oval mirror in her walk-in closet. She admired the flow of the green silk negligee against her body, but she couldn't look at her face. She was too disgusted with herself.

About last night...

About sleeping with Simon Kramer. What had she been thinking? Sure, she'd spent the past two years wondering what it would be like. But it would have been safer to just keep wondering.

Because being with him...

That had been a lot more powerful than she'd ever imagined it could be. The man was incredible. His body, the way he'd touched her, the way he'd moved inside her.

She shivered. But she wasn't really cold. Heat suffused her body, as it had every time she'd thought of the night before, of what she and Simon Kramer had done in his office, on his couch.

How many other women had he taken against the supple black leather? She hadn't thought about that in the incredible heat of the moment. But she'd been thinking about it ever since...

Not that she wanted to be anything special to him. She didn't want to be *anything* to him. She didn't even want to see him again.

That was partially why she'd called in sick, which was another reason she couldn't look at her face in the mirror. She was disgusted with herself for lying and for being a coward. She was tougher than that; if she wasn't, she wouldn't have made it on her own all these years in New York.

Maybe it was better that she didn't go into the office because then she wouldn't have to endure the humiliation of being walked out with her box of belongings. And she had no doubt that Simon would walk her to the door. He had no use for her anymore, not after last night.

Her doorbell rang, and she tensed. Who could that be? Hardly anyone had her new address yet. She still hadn't unpacked all her boxes, which was another reason she'd decided not to go into the office today. She had too much to do. But the box of lingerie samples had distracted her, and she'd found herself trying on some of the things. She'd wanted inspiration for more designs but all she could think about was Simon and last night.

The doorbell rang again, insistently, as if someone had her or his finger pressed against it. How had the visitor even gotten past the doorman? This wasn't like her old building in Queens that had a broken lock on the door to the lobby, so there had been absolutely no security but for her overprotective neighbors and the two roommates with whom she'd shared the two-bedroom apartment.

Thank goodness for them.

Maybe she hadn't survived entirely on her own in the city. But this building, in the Garment District, was supposed to have high security, at least that was what the property manager had claimed. So maybe it was a new neighbor introducing her or himself, which would be nice since no one had been particularly friendly or warm yet.

At least she had one friend in the building, the one who'd recommended the place to her. But Muriel was out of town on a photo shoot. If Bette hadn't had to work out these two weeks, she could have gone with her.

Damn Simon Kramer and his employment contract. No matter that Bette was doing better financially than she ever had, she still couldn't afford a lawsuit that she was certain to lose.

She grabbed a long fleece robe from a hook on the closet wall before heading through her bedroom, with the sheets tangled on the unmade bed, to the living room. The sun shone through the tall windows in the brick walls, casting a warm glow on the dark-stained hardwood floor. She loved this place. But she wasn't entirely convinced it was as safe as the property manager and Muriel had claimed.

How had someone found out where she lived? Unless Muriel had sent congratulatory flowers for Bette quitting Street Legal. Or had Simon sent the kiss-off flowers he'd sent to every other lover he'd tired of?

But Simon didn't know where she lived.

To be safe, Bette paused before opening the door. She rose up on tiptoe and peered through the peephole. And her breath caught in her lungs as fear filled her.

No...

How the hell had he found out where she lived? And how had he gotten inside the building? But then she knew. He had somehow charmed his way inside, just like he'd charmed his way inside her the night before.

Abandoning the button for the bell, he pounded on the door instead. "Bette, I know you're inside, and I'm not leaving until you let me in."

She didn't doubt that he would keep ringing her bell and pounding on the door until she did. And if she ever wanted the neighbors to warm up to her, she shouldn't risk alienating any of them with a noise disturbance.

With a sigh, she turned the dead bolt and opened the door. "What are you doing here?" she asked as she leaned against the jamb, blocking his way inside.

But she didn't deter him. He put his hands on her shoulders and moved her aside so he could enter. "Simon!" She gasped. But she closed the door behind him.

"Don't you mean how?" he asked. "You didn't change your address with HR."

HR was a couple of women who handled payroll and benefits. He was really Human Resources, the one who personally interviewed and hired all applicants. Her face flushed at the thought of him asking those gossipy women where she lived.

"Then how?" she asked.

"One of your former roommates gave me your good news."

She tensed. What roommate? And what exactly had he told him? She was afraid to ask so she returned to her original question. "Why?"

He grinned. "John Paul couldn't resist my charm."

John Paul. He had probably fallen in love with Simon at first sight. But JP loved her, too, so he wouldn't have revealed too much information. He'd probably only told Simon where she was because the guy was a hopeless romantic.

Bette was too practical for romance. Or at least

that was what she'd always thought until last night and that romantic candlelit dinner Simon had catered for them.

"Why are you here?" she asked. That was the question she really wanted him to answer. Did he want more the way she did?

"I should have tracked you down last night," he said, "after you ran out the way you did."

Her face heated with embarrassment. She had acted like a fool, thinking she could act. That had been stupid. "It was late," she said. "And I was too drunk to work." Maybe he would think that was why she'd done what she had, undressing for him.

"I'm here to bring you to work," he said. "You still have nine days to go on your two-week notice—if you still want to leave."

Her already racing pulse quickened even more with surprise. "You still want me there?"

He stared down at her, and his blue eyes darkened. Then his gaze skimmed down her body, over her fleece robe, as if he could see right through it.

Her nipples tightened in reaction, and heat rushed to her core. She'd never wanted anyone the way she wanted him. And that had been before she'd even known how he felt inside her and how much pleasure he could give her.

"I definitely still want you," he said, and there was no mistaking the intent in his deep, sensual voice.

"But—but that's not your usual MO," she protested.

"Usual MO?" he asked as he arched a dark blond brow. "What is my usual MO?"

Maybe she was still a little buzzed from the wine the night before or the sex, because her filter was off again. She answered him honestly, "You're notorious for being the king of one-night stands."

He didn't deny it; he just chuckled. "Is that why you ran out the way you did last night?"

She nodded. "And since we had one night…"

"You thought that was all I would want?"

Realizing she should have used more tact, she sank her teeth into her bottom lip and just nodded her head.

He stepped closer, until his body pressed against hers. And dropping his voice to a low, sexy whisper, he murmured, "One night with you would never be enough."

She gasped as her core began to throb with desire for him. And he took her mouth, kissing her deeply. His tongue slid between her lips, like his cock had slid inside her last night. His hands moved to her shoulders again, but he didn't move her aside this time. He pulled her closer.

Her breasts crushed against his chest; her heart pounded madly—in perfect rhythm with his. Just like they'd been last night…

That rhythm had been fast and frantic, though, as they'd both lost control. She couldn't lose control

again the way she had before. She had to remember
who and what he was: Simon Kramer, heartbreaking
charmer and ruthless attorney.

CHAPTER SIX

SIMON LIFTED HIS head from hers and tried to clear it. He needed to focus on anything other than her beautiful face. She wasn't wearing her glasses today. She probably wore no makeup, either, but her pale skin was flawless, her lashes long and thick and as deep a brown as her hair. She didn't need makeup, not with her natural beauty.

Apparently, she didn't need her glasses, either. At least not all the time. But until last night he'd never seen her without them. Were they necessary? Or just part of her disguise?

He felt like she'd been wearing one the past two years. Like she'd deliberately been trying to mislead him about who she really was.

Because he'd had no idea how hot she was, how wet and responsive...

He suppressed a groan that burned the back of his throat, like she'd burned him up the night before with her passion. Who the hell was Bette Monroe really?

Her hair was down, too, falling in long, rich, brown waves around her slender shoulders. Even with the long fleece robe covering up her substantial curves, she was damn sexy. Then the sash of that robe slipped out of its loose knot, and the fleece parted to reveal dark green silk and lace.

His breath escaped in a gasp, like he'd been sucker punched. Not that he knew what that felt like. Nobody had ever sucker punched him before. He was always too aware, too prepared, to get suckered.

Until now.

Until Bette Monroe.

"What the hell are you wearing?" he asked, his voice gruff with desire.

Her face flushed with embarrassment, and her fingers trembled as she fumbled with the sash, trying to retie the fleece robe.

He caught her fingers in his and tugged the sash free of the loops. Then he pushed the robe from her shoulders. Her bare shoulders...

He wasn't certain how the hell the negligee wasn't slipping right off her body. Then he noticed another bow on her back, tied between her shoulder blades. If he undid that bow, the negligee would drop to her feet. His fingers twitched. He wanted to untie that bow so badly.

But that was probably her plan, keep him so sexually charged that he couldn't think straight, so that he wouldn't catch her in the act of stealing case files. Why else was she wearing lingerie around the house?

Unless...

He glanced around the apartment. "Are you

alone?" Or had she stayed home because she was entertaining a lover?

Her brow furrowed slightly. "Yes, I live here alone. I don't have a roommate."

"Then how can you afford this place?" There were doors off the main living room, so it had at least one bedroom. Street Legal paid their employees well enough that she should have been able to afford more than that tiny two-bedroom in Queens that John Paul had admitted they'd shared with another roommate, apparently his boyfriend.

So maybe she'd saved up some of that money but she couldn't have saved enough to be able to pay the rent for a one-bedroom in the Garment District with a full kitchen. She actually had full-size appliances, not just a two-burner stove top and half-size fridge like she'd shared with John Paul and his partner. There was also a big bay window where a table would fit if she had one. She didn't. But then she'd obviously just moved in. Boxes sat on the hardwood floor. Maybe that was why she'd called in to work— so she could unpack.

He looked back at her and arched a brow as he waited for her answer.

She narrowed her eyes and glared at him. "That's really not any of your business."

He nearly growled in frustration. "That's what you said about your reason for resigning."

"I don't have to give you one," she reminded him. "Your own contract says that." She gestured to where the document was laid out on her reclaimed-wood coffee table. While the place wasn't totally furnished, he liked the pieces she had. He liked her taste but not just in furniture.

He could taste her on his lips yet. She tasted like some kind of citrusy tea and dark chocolate. A cup and a piece of foil with chocolate crumbs on it sat atop the coffee table, as well.

"Why don't you want to give me one?" he asked. Usually people told him why they were quitting. *I'm in love with you and I know you'll never love me back.*

It's too hard to work with you.

You expect too much.

Bette had claimed none of those reasons. In fact, she'd never complained about the workload or about him. So why did she want to leave?

"Like I told you before," she replied, "it's my business. Not yours."

"You didn't mind my being in your business last night," he reminded her as he stepped closer again. "I was all up in your business…"

And he wanted to be all up inside her again.

Her lips parted on a gasp as she stared up at him. She wanted him to; she had to after last night, after how incredible it had been.

Or hadn't she felt it?

He'd never lost control like that before, had never come so quickly. Usually he made sure his partner had many, many orgasms before he found his own release.

He wanted her to be as out of control and crazy as she'd made him the night before. So he reached for that bow between her shoulder blades. The bodice of the long negligee loosened and released her full breasts before it pooled like a green silk puddle around her bare feet.

She was bare all over. She didn't even wear panties beneath that gown. And he was damn glad of that. His hand was shaking so badly he wasn't certain that he could have untied another bow. Not that he figured all her panties were made that way. But he wanted to find out.

"Why are you so damn sexy?"

Her mouth curved into a smile. "It's the lingerie."

He reached out and traced his fingertips over the curve of her breast, then over her flat stomach to the curve of her hip and ass. "You're not wearing anything right now." But that sexy smile. "And you're gorgeous."

She sighed. "When you turn on the charm like that…"

"What?" he asked. Did he tempt her to reveal all her secrets? To admit that she'd betrayed him?

"You make me crazy," she murmured. And she reached for him. After pushing his suit jacket from his shoulders, she attacked the buttons on his shirt, frantically freeing them. And each inch of his chest she revealed, she pressed her lips against in silky kisses. Then her tongue flicked over his nipple.

And he groaned. She was the one making him crazy, making him lose control. But he couldn't risk that again. He was the one who was supposed to be seducing her.

Besides the coffee table, she had a couch—thankfully—or he would have taken her on the table. The couch was big and deep, nearly the size of a bed with soft cushions and pillows. He pushed her onto it and followed her down.

And he went down on her. He didn't just taste her like he had the night before. He feasted on her. While he used one hand to massage her breast and tease the nipple, he used the other on her pussy. As he slid his fingers inside her wet core, he nibbled and sucked on her clit.

She screamed as she came. And he lapped up her sweet release.

He groaned. And damn it, his control snapped again. He had to be inside her, had to be in all that wet heat. He shucked his pants and briefs and fumbled with the condom. She took the packet from him and tore it open. Then she rolled it over his pulsating cock. He nearly came as she pumped him through the latex. But he wasn't having it…

He was having her. So he dragged off her hand and spun her around. Then with her clutching the back of the couch cushions, he moved his dick between her legs. As he stroked her ass, he found her core and slid inside her. Then he cupped her breasts, rolling her nipples between his fingers and thumbs while he thrust inside her.

She arched her luscious hips and took him deeper, grinding against his groin as she sought her orgasm. She came again with a scream of pleasure. His balls ached, stretching as they filled. Then he found his release.

She came again before he pulled out. Her inner muscles clutched him as she whimpered with pleasure. He hated to separate. But he had to clean up. He found the bathroom through the first doorway off the living room. After disposing of the condom and washing up, he came back to find her lying limply against her couch cushions.

Her glorious breasts rose and fell and shimmied as she panted for breath.

"Are you trying to make me fall in love with you?" she asked breathlessly as she stared up at him with those big dark eyes of hers.

He waited for the panic he usually felt when someone professed feelings for him he knew he'd never return. And when he noticed how closely she watched him, he wondered if she was looking for that panic, too.

He grinned and replied, "Just trying to get you to work."

Instead of looking hurt or even disappointed, she laughed and sat up. "All right. I'll shower and come into the office." She gestured toward the door. "I'm sure you can show yourself out."

He had no intention of leaving.

Yet.

Bette should have gone into the office that morning. But then she had never imagined that Simon Kramer would track her down at home. Not that she would ever feel entirely at home in her new place, especially now that he'd been inside it with her. That he'd been inside her.

She'd showered but she could still smell him on her skin. Just like he'd been in her body, he was inside her head, as well. But she wouldn't let him into her heart. Despite what she'd said to him, she knew better than to fall for a man like Simon Kramer.

He would break her heart for certain. But hell, that would probably be better than falling for some man who wanted to keep her heart. Or her...

Like the men for whom her mom and sister had fallen. Dad had forced Mom to give up all her dreams and live his as the preacher of a small-town church. Her mother had once been wild and full of fun. But Bette had never seen that except in the old photo albums her mother had hidden where she hadn't thought anyone would look.

Her sister should have known better, but she'd fallen for a man just like their self-righteous father. A youth minister—and she lived the same quiet, boring life their mother lived.

Bette shook her head in disgust of their choices. Of course they acted like they were disgusted with hers, especially her father. He'd disowned her years ago. At least Mom and Sissy still sent her cards on her birthday.

Carrying her heels, she hurried out of her bedroom. She needed to get to the office quickly or Simon might return for her. But apparently, he hadn't left because she found him standing over her coffee table. She dropped her shoes and pressed a hand against her madly pounding heart. "You scared me!" she said.

He glanced up as if he'd been caught unawares, too. And he almost looked guilty. What had he been doing while she'd been showering? She'd left the employment contract lying out on the coffee table. But he wouldn't have to read that over; he'd written it.

That wasn't all she'd left out in the living room, though. Her purse was lying beside the table. But he wouldn't have been going through that. Would he? It wasn't as if Simon Kramer needed to steal any cash from her wallet. She didn't carry much else in it but some makeup and her checkbook.

She hadn't shaken all of her damn old-fashioned, small-town upbringing because she was too cautious to do everything online. Or maybe she needed the checkbook because she needed the peace of mind of keeping track of everything she spent and earned. And finally, after years of barely getting by in the city, she was getting those things in the right order. She was finally earning more than she spent.

"I thought you left," she said. "I told you I would meet you at the office."

"And I thought I better wait for you," he said.

For what? Another romp on her couch? Her heart flipped at the thought but then she noticed his face. There was no disarming grin. No teasing twinkle in his blue eyes. He didn't trust her for some reason and she felt that it was more than her calling in sick.

"You didn't need to do that," she said. "I know you're busy."

He was so busy that she was surprised he'd taken the time to track down where she was, let alone wait for her after he'd done that—after he'd done her.

"I am busy," he said. "That's why I needed to make sure you didn't have a sudden relapse of whatever illness you claimed was keeping you from coming into the office today."

She faked a cough, then laughed as he glared at her. Unintimidated, she pressed the back of her hand to her forehead. "I am feeling a little warm still…" But that was because of him, because even though he'd dressed, she could still see him gloriously naked. He was so damn good-looking. It wasn't fair. It really wasn't.

"Don't try to con a con," he warned her, and his eyes were as cold and hard as they'd been the day he'd found her leaving the resignation letter in his office.

"Con?" she uneasily repeated as a chill chased down her spine. "Are you admitting that you're a con artist?"

Was he not even really a lawyer? She'd seen his college degree and law license framed on his office wall. But that didn't mean they hadn't been forged. As infamous as Street Legal was, someone would have discovered if the managing partner was a con artist. Wouldn't they?

He shook his head. "I wouldn't call myself a con artist," he said. "Not anymore. But I still recognize a con."

She smiled and assured him, "I'm not trying to con you." But could he say the same?

What exactly would he have to con out of her, though? Sex? She'd given that freely enough. No con required. He hadn't even had to pile on the charm very much, except for the compliments he'd given her.

"When were you a con artist?" she asked. "And why would you tell me that?" Obviously, he was onto her little game of pretending to fall for him. But now he'd made it a challenge for her to be able to convince him.

He shrugged. "It's not exactly a secret that my partners and I were teenage runaways. To survive on the streets, I had to run a con or two."

Shock gripped her. "You really did grow up on the streets?"

He nodded.

"I thought that was just a story that PR firm concocted to make you guys sound glamorous."

Over the past two years, she'd personally witnessed how fast and loose McCann Public Relations, and Allison McCann in particular, played with the truth.

Simon laughed now. "Glamorous? There was nothing glamorous about that life. But we weren't going to lie about where we came from, so Allison decided it would be smarter to make the most of it."

Allison.

Resentment churned in Bette's stomach. She wasn't a fan of the owner of McCann Public Relations. The woman was cold and ruthless. And so beautiful that there was no way any man would have gone two years without noticing her. Not that Bette was jealous or anything.

She would have rather had Simon never notice her at all. Now she was the liar. She knew that wasn't the case or she would have never experienced the most mind-blowing sex of her life. What they'd done...

How he'd made her feel...

He'd made her crazy with desire and then with pleasure.

"I'm not conning you," she said. At least not about calling in sick. "I didn't come into the office today because I really didn't think you'd want to see me again after last night."

"Is that why you ran out while I was in the bathroom?" he asked.

She nodded. Despite his warning, she had to try

to con him in order to get him to release her from that contract. "I also didn't want to risk seeing you again."

He narrowed his eyes—those gorgeous blue eyes—and his brow furrowed with suspicion. "What's the risk, Bette?"

"My heart," she told him and forced a shaky sigh. "I'm worried I'm going to fall for you." As she uttered the words, they didn't ring as hollowly as she'd thought they would. And she actually felt a twinge of fear.

But she couldn't—she wouldn't—fall for Simon Kramer. There really was no risk at all.

Was there?

CHAPTER SEVEN

WHO THE HELL was Bette Monroe? The shy woman
with the glasses and her hair in a bun? Or the sexy
siren in naughty lingerie?

He studied her across the small space between
their seats in the back of the town car. She was wearing the glasses again, and her hair was all bound up.
He suspected that was just a disguise—an act, like
her worry that she was going to fall for him.

Just a few nights ago she had laughed when he'd
asked if she loved him. So what had changed since
then?

They'd had sex a couple of times. He was good.
But he wasn't that good, not good enough to make
her fall for him just because he'd given her some
pleasure. While other women had professed as much,
Bette was different. Those women had already been
half in love with him because of who he was and
what he had: a hell of a reputation and bank account.

Bette had never seemed very impressed with
either. But then she claimed money didn't matter to
her. That even if he gave her a raise, she wouldn't

stay working for Street Legal. He knew why now that he'd gotten a look at her checkbook. She'd made some recent deposits. Some pretty damn good ones.

She had to be the mole.

A pressure settled heavily on his chest with disappointment—which was weird. He should be relieved that he'd found the mole. Now he would be able to stop any more information leaks. He would be able to stop her.

All he had to do was fire her and block her access to Street Legal. Delete her passwords, change the locks.

She wouldn't be able to sell any more of their information. But somehow it didn't feel right. Maybe she'd received that money another way.

An inheritance...

"What?" she asked as she lifted her hand to her mouth like she had the night before. "Do I have something on my teeth? Lipstick smeared?"

"Not yet," he said. But he wanted to smear it. Hell, he wanted it smeared on his cock as she sucked him off.

Her lips curved slightly. "Then what is it?" she asked. "Why are you staring at me?"

She really had no idea how beautiful she was. "I'm trying to figure you out," he admitted.

She tilted her head and studied him as intently as he'd been studying her. "You wonder how I could fall for you when I laughed the other night when you asked if I was in love with you?"

He laughed now. "That's the least of my questions about you, Bette."

She sighed. "Are you still wondering why I'm quitting?"

"Wondering..." He laughed again. "That's putting it a little mildly." He was more than curious. He was desperate to know her reason.

"I don't know why you care," she said.

"I want to know what your better offer is," he said. "To see if I can match it."

"I already told you it's not about money."

"Why?" he asked. "Do you have family money? A trust fund or inheritance you just got access to?"

She laughed. "My father is the minister of a very small church in a very small town in Michigan. If he and my mom didn't have housing provided by the parish, they wouldn't be able to afford groceries."

"Your mom doesn't work?" he asked.

She shook her head, and her lips curled slightly with disgust. "Being his wife is her full-time job."

So those deposits in her bank account hadn't come from her parents. Bette Monroe was no trust fund baby. Where the hell had she gotten that money?

He could think of one place. Their opposition in court.

"She's a loyal wife," he murmured. As far as he knew, his parents hadn't been married. He didn't even remember his mother. According to his father, she'd abandoned them. But that didn't mean it was true. His father hadn't had any idea how to be honest. It had always been easier for him to lie than tell the truth. "That's commendable."

Bette sighed. "It's sad."

"So you're not looking to get married anytime soon?"

She opened her mouth. And he expected an adamant *no* to come out of her lips. But then it was as if she caught herself and forced out a wistful sigh instead. "I would have said no," she admitted, "a few days ago..."

"What's changed?" he asked.

"You." She slid forward and dropped to her knees on the floor between their seats, and she was between his legs. "You've changed. You notice me now."

"You're kind of hard to miss," he murmured. And he wondered again what the hell she was up to...even as he was up again, his dick hardening and pushing against the fly of his pants.

Even though he couldn't trust her, he wanted her. But then he couldn't trust anyone. So it didn't matter much. He just knew that he would never be able to trust her.

Bette glanced at the dark glass separating the front seat from the back seats. There was no way the driver could see back there. Was there?

Did she care?

As a preacher's daughter, she should. But hell, Daddy had consigned her to hell long ago when she'd professed her love of fashion over bible studies. And she didn't consider pleasure the sin that Daddy did.

She'd never felt as much pleasure as she had with Simon Kramer. And she knew it was going to end soon like all of his liaisons did. She was unsettling him with her actions and her words. While he was off balance, Bette wanted to push him over the edge, to the madness that he'd driven her to just a short time ago on her couch.

So she stayed on her knees between his legs, and she reached for the zipper on his pants. His breath hissed out with the sound of the metal sliding down as she lowered his zipper. She pushed aside the fine cotton material of his briefs and freed his penis. It pulsated and vibrated in her touch, veins bulging on it like the veins bulging on his neck as he arched his head back.

"Bette…" Her name was just a groan on his lips. "What are you doing?"

She peeked up at him through her lashes. "You don't know? And here I thought you were the experienced one."

He narrowed his eyes and stared down at her. "You're really a preacher's daughter?" he asked, and there was skepticism in his deep voice.

"I'm the black sheep," she admitted. "The one who left for the big city and a life of sex and drugs." Even though it was what her family believed, she laughed like it was all a joke. "Since I'm not into drugs, I guess I will have to settle for the sex."

"You should never settle," he told her.

She felt the same way, that her mom and sister had settled for security. But in that security, they were insecure because they had no idea who they were anymore. Because they had had to change so much for their partners.

If Bette ever really fell for anyone, he would have to love and respect her for who she was and not try to change her to fit into his life. Not that she wanted to fall for anyone.

So she didn't risk settling for a person, she'd rather just settle for sex. But sex with Simon wasn't a consolation prize. It was the grand prize.

Like most lottery winners who couldn't make the money last, she knew the pleasure would eventually end, as well. So she had to make the most of it. The most of her time with him...

She lowered her mouth and closed it over the tip of his penis. It moved against her tongue, which she swirled around the girth of him.

He groaned and reached out, tangling his fingers in her hair. She'd have to redo the pins later because she felt some slip free. But she didn't care.

She didn't care about anything but driving him crazy.

He was too big for her to take all of him in her mouth. So she used her hands, too, sliding them up and down the length of him while she sucked on the head. Then she'd draw in a deep breath and take him as deep as she could manage in her throat.

Teasing him...

His hands moved from her hair to her shoulders and gripped them as if trying to pull her up from her knees. "Bette, you're killing me..."

With his cock in her mouth, she looked up at him. Then she swirled her tongue around the tip.

And that control he seemed so reluctant to let go of must have snapped again. He arched his hips with the need to thrust. So she took him deeper in her throat.

Then she slid her mouth up and down him.

His hands gripped her shoulders as his body tensed, and a deep growl sounded as if it was torn from his throat. Then he came, hot and sweet on her tongue.

She licked him from her lips and smiled up at him.

He stared down at her, his eyes still dark with the dilated pupils swallowing the blue like she'd swallowed him. He shook his head.

"What?" she asked.

"How could I work so closely with you for two years and know nothing about you?"

"You didn't ask," she reminded him.

"Would it have mattered if I did? You're not inclined to answer the other questions I ask you." He tucked himself back into his briefs and pulled up his zipper and shook his head again as if he was unable to believe what had just happened.

And she was unable to believe that it hadn't happened before. Women probably gave him blow jobs in back seats all the time. He was that damn gorgeous...

And irresistible.

She licked her lips again, loving the taste of him. Loving that she gave him that pleasure. And maybe that was what had taken him aback, that mousy Bette Monroe would do something like that. That was what kids had called her in school. She'd even been dubbed that in fashion college because she hadn't had the piercings and tattoos, or worn the wild clothes her classmates had.

But what she designed wasn't meant to be seen by everyone. Just the women who wore them and the men those women cared about enough to show.

She'd showed Simon more of her designs than she had other men. But it wasn't because she cared about him. That wasn't why.

"You remind me of the *Mona Lisa*," he said.

She laughed. "What?"

"It's obvious in that painting that she has some salacious secret," he said. "And it's obvious that you do, too."

"I guess we share a salacious secret now," she murmured as she stroked her finger across her bottom lip.

He groaned. "Damn it…"

"What?"

"You just made me hard again," he admitted. "And I wouldn't have thought that would be possible yet…"

Neither had she. But she was kind of glad that he was—because her pulse was pounding in her core, demanding release from the tension pleasing him had given her. She wanted to feel what he had, wanted the pleasure they gave each other.

And now he was the one sliding off his seat onto

his knees on the floor between them. But even on his knees, he was taller than she was sitting. So he had to lean down to kiss her. His mouth sliding back and forth across hers. He groaned, probably because he could taste himself on her lips.

She touched him, moving her hand from his chest to his groin. And sure enough his cock was pressing against his fly again—long and hard and hot. She smiled against his lips.

"Siren," he murmured.

She lifted her head and listened. "I don't hear anything."

His mouth curved into a slight grin. "You," he said. "You're the siren."

"The mermaid who lures sailors to their deaths?" she asked. "I'm not sure that's a compliment."

He laughed. "Oh, it's not a good thing," he agreed. "At least not for me." His fingers shook a little as he moved them to the buttons of her cardigan. "Ever since you walked out of your bedroom all dressed up like this, I've been dying to know what you're wearing underneath."

But he took his time with each button, undoing them slowly as if he was building up the anticipation. That was probably how he unwrapped presents, as well—slowly to savor them.

But as a runaway growing up on the streets, had he had presents? How had he survived let alone thrived like he had?

She didn't know him as well as she'd thought she had. There was much more to him than his charm and his ruthlessness—because now she understood why he had both.

For survival…

She wasn't sure she would survive his slow, sweet torture of her. At last, he parted her sweater and pushed it from her shoulders. Then his breath hissed out between his teeth.

"Damn, Bette…"

She'd put on another bustier instead of a camisole. This one was leather, with cups, and of course her signature bow. It was tied at the bottom of the leather strap that bound the bustier together.

"Where the hell do you find this stuff?" he asked. "I've never seen anything as sexy."

Pride suffused her. She could have told him he'd never seen it before because she'd designed it. But he would be seeing it soon since she would have her own line at the fashion house for the premier retailer of lingerie in the country.

He was already so surprised that she wore lingerie that she didn't know if she was flattered or offended. If he laughed, like so many other people had, when she said she designed it, she would definitely be offended. So offended that it would be impossible to work out the rest of her notice for him.

Unless she could get him to cut that notice short…

But then he untied that bustier and released her breasts so he could play with them, and she wasn't so certain she wanted to cut that notice short anymore. Because that would mean cutting short the pleasure he gave her…

And he gave her pleasure now.

While he suckled on one of her nipples, he moved his hand beneath her skirt. He pushed aside her panties and slid his fingers inside her. She was already wet and ready for him. When he moved his thumb over her clit, she came, crying out his name.

And he cursed.

Blinking away the desire, she stared up at him.

"We're at the office," he told her, his voice gruff with desire and disappointment. "We'll have to finish this later."

Her hands were shaking so badly that he had to bind her back into the bustier and button her sweater back up. But he did it, even as a muscle twitched in his cheek—just above his tightly clenched jaw.

"Definitely a siren," he murmured.

She wasn't one. But she heard one, a warning that she was getting in too deep with him. So she was almost honest when she said, "I really think I could care for you."

But she wouldn't let that happen. She wouldn't let herself fall for anyone, least of all someone as ruthless and charming as Simon Kramer.

CHAPTER EIGHT

DESPITE HAVING THE partner meeting every Tuesday morning, Simon had nearly forgotten about it. But a lot had happened in the past week.

A lot of sex with Bette. A hell of a lot of crazy, mind-blowing sex. That was the reason he'd nearly forgotten the meeting. Losing his memory was probably a side effect of having his mind blown so often and so completely that he'd nearly forgotten the reason he'd begun the seduction of Bette Monroe. He'd nearly forgotten that she was the office mole.

Probably.

He still had no proof. Sure, he'd gotten a look at her checkbook. But those deposits could have come from something else. Maybe she'd sold something other than that information from their case files.

Like her body...

He would certainly pay if she started charging him. She was so damn passionate and sexy and generous.

And distracting.

He needed to focus on finding evidence. Real evidence. Because right now he had nothing but his suspicions.

Apparently, he wasn't the only one with suspicions. Ronan and Trevor studied him through narrowed eyes. And Stone wouldn't even look at him as if he was too disgusted.

"What?" he asked them.

"We heard about you and your assistant," Ronan said.

Now he knew why Stone wouldn't look at him. "Thanks a hell of a lot," he told his friend.

Stone shook his head. "I didn't tell them."

"You knew?" Trevor asked.

"Yeah…"

"And you didn't stop him from risking the whole damn practice getting sued?" Trevor asked.

"She's not going to sue me," Simon assured them, although maybe he should have been worried about that. If she would steal secrets from them, why wouldn't she sue?

Stone sighed. "I'm not as sure as you are about that. Just because she's given her notice—"

"She's given her notice?" Ronan asked. Then he groaned. "Damn it, we're certain to get sued if she's quitting over sexual harassment."

"I'm not harassing her," Simon said.

"But you are sleeping with her," Ronan said.

They had never actually slept together. But they'd had a hell of a lot of sex.

"Everybody's talking about it," Trevor said.

So much for him and Bette sharing a secret, their salacious one. He glared at Stone. "What—you've been gossiping like a little old lady?"

"I've got a hell of a lot more important things to worry about than your love life," Stone said.

Simon's heart slammed against his ribs. Love life? Hardly.

"You're not in love, are you?" Ronan asked.

Simon's heart slammed against his ribs and he exclaimed, "Of course not!"

"Then what the hell are you up to?" Trevor asked.

"I'm trying to find out if she's the mole," Simon admitted.

The color drained from Stone's face. "You didn't tell me that."

He sighed. "Because I don't know for sure if she is. I need proof."

"Why do you even suspect her?" Ronan asked.

"Because she's leaving," he said. And because of some of things he'd seen in her purse, specifically in her checkbook, like the ATM receipt for the deposit of a big check. The slip had also shown that she carried a very healthy balance. No wonder she'd been able to afford her new place. And she'd admitted she hadn't inherited any money or come into a trust.

"So?" Ronan said. "That doesn't prove her guilt."

"I got close to her so I could find proof," Simon admitted. But he felt a pang of guilt over that. What if she wasn't the mole? And what if she was starting to care for him like she'd been warning him she was?

Then he'd been seducing and using her for no reason. No. There was pleasure. More than pleasure.

"Have you found any proof?" Trevor asked skeptically.

Maybe he knew that Simon had gotten sidetracked—with her beauty, with the sex...

The incredible, mind-blowing sex. She was the most responsive and generous lover he'd ever had. And the way they moved together, the way they fitted...

She matched him in a way he'd never been matched before, but he was worried that it wasn't just with sex. Not that he was falling for her or anything. These unsettling feelings he had for her weren't anything more than desire and attraction and suspicion. Maybe she didn't just match him as a lover but as a con, too.

"Nothing that would hold up in court," he said. And because these were his friends, he was honest with them and admitted, "But she's come into some money. She's moved. She's bought stuff."

Her lingerie collection alone probably cost a fortune. The materials were decadent and the designs were works of art. But to him, the outfits were just like a light bulb showing off the work of art that was her perfect body.

"Maybe she inherited some money," Trevor said.

He shook his head. "I checked around." He hadn't just taken her word for it. "She's not been anyone's heir."

"Mistress?" Ronan asked.

Anger surged through Simon. "Of course you'd think that." He had, too. But when would she have time for a man—even a married one—with as much time as she'd been spending with Simon?

Ronan snorted. "I'm a divorce lawyer. Of course I'd think that. And you, being the con, would think she's the mole. But it doesn't track."

"Why not?"

"I agree that it makes no sense," Stone said. "If she's making money off us, why would she leave?"

The others nodded in agreement. They didn't understand a con the way Simon did.

The trick was to get out before getting caught. He figured that had been her intention. But it was too late for her now. He'd caught her. He just needed the evidence to prove it. To his partners and to the police and to himself. He didn't want to believe that it was her. Still, it was the only thing that made sense— for her leaving and for her coming into that money.

As much as he'd wished it wasn't true, he had to face the fact that she'd conned him. He wasn't buying that she was falling for him—no matter how many times she'd claimed that she was.

He wasn't sure which con he was more pissed about: her selling information from their case files or trying to make him believe she might genuinely care about him.

A sudden chill raced down Bette's spine and raised goose bumps on her skin. She shivered and glanced up from the computer monitor she'd been studying and discovered three men standing in her small office.

Why were all of Simon's partners paying her a visit? Like Simon, they had barely paid her any attention the two years she'd worked for Street Legal.

"Can I help you?" she asked.

Unlike Simon, they were all dark haired. Ronan Hall's hair was black. Stone Michaelsen's was dark brown like hers and Trevor Sinclair's was more of an auburn. They were also all bigger than Simon. The three of them barely fitted into her office, their broad shoulders rubbing against each other's.

How had they entered so quietly?

They'd lived on the streets. Maybe they'd learned to be quiet there. Or maybe she'd just been too distracted with thoughts of their managing partner to notice if an entire circus had entered her office, riding elephants while juggling rings of fire.

"You can stay," Trevor Sinclair suggested.

"Simon told you that I gave my notice," she said and leaned back in her chair.

Maybe one of them could convince him to let her go early. She only had four days—including today—left on her notice. She could last four days.

Couldn't she?

But she was already boneless from all the pleasure he'd given her. She didn't want to lose her backbone completely the way her mom and her sister had. She didn't want to get addicted to him and desperate and clingy like all of his other ex-lovers. No. The less time she spent with Simon Kramer the better. At least, the safer...for her.

"Why are you leaving?" Ronan Hall asked.

She hadn't told Simon; she damn well was not going to tell him, either. She just shook her head. "This just isn't a good fit."

Stone Michaelsen studied her like she was one of the criminals he represented. As she'd told Simon, quitting was not a crime.

"Street Legal or Simon?" he asked.

Heat rushed to her face. She and Simon fitted together perfectly, like her body had been made for his. But then his body was so perfect that she couldn't imagine him not fitting with every woman he seduced.

Had he actually seduced her? Or had she seduced him?

"I don't have a background in law," she said. "I am really not a good fit as a legal assistant." So why had Simon hired her two years ago?

The three men exchanged a glance as if they were all wondering the same thing. From the way Ronan glanced down her body, it was clear he had his suspicions. He wasn't wrong about them—now.

But she knew that wasn't why Simon had hired her since he hadn't even noticed her until she'd given him her notice.

"You must have done a fine job the past two

years," Stone said, "or Simon wouldn't have kept you."

Now her embarrassment gave way to annoyance. Simon did not own her. He never had and he never would. No man owned Bette Monroe. Instead of telling his partners those thoughts, she just offered them a tight smile.

"We hate to have you leave," Trevor said. But he didn't sound particularly sincere. In fact, he sounded suspicious, and he studied her with a strange look on his face, kind of like the look that had been on Simon's when she'd caught him in her apartment.

Actually, Simon had looked both suspicious and guilty that day, like she'd caught him doing something. Rummaging through her things? Her purse?

Had he seen any of her designs?

She doubted it. Those were on the desk in her bedroom, and she didn't think he'd gone in there while she'd been showering. And he hadn't been back to her apartment since that day—except for in her thoughts.

She kept imagining him there.

She kept imagining him everywhere but most especially inside her. It was almost as if she could feel him in there, filling her completely.

Heat rushed to her face again and pooled lower in her body, between her legs. She crossed them and clenched her thighs together, but that only intensified the sensation. She needed Simon again.

No. Four more days was too many. She was too

close to getting addicted to him, to becoming desperate and needy for him like all those other women he'd dumped.

"If you all feel like I should leave now, I understand," Bette told them. "If you're worried about the confidentiality with your clients."

"Should we be worried?" Stone asked.

"Yeah," Ronan said, "it's not like you're going to work for the opposition or anything, is it?"

She shook her head. "No. Like I told you, I'm not suited at all for a job in law." Her passion was fashion. For years that was the only real passion she'd had.

Now there was Simon. But he wasn't just a passion. He was becoming an obsession, as well. She needed to get away from him as soon as possible.

But his partners were no help. "You're welcome to stay," Stone told her. "As long as you'd like."

She'd like to leave now. For some reason she hesitated to admit it. And they were gone before she could form the words. It was only four more days. Four more days of Simon Kramer...

She wasn't really falling for him, though. She couldn't. She knew him too well.

Didn't she?

CHAPTER NINE

How could Bette have worked for him for two years and Simon still know so little about her? When he'd hired her, he'd checked her references and résumé. But now he had to pull up her employment file again to refresh his memory. She'd worked in fashion houses before she'd worked for Street Legal. Her degree was in fashion.

He'd dated a couple of design assistants. They didn't make much. That was the reason he'd figured she'd quit the fashion house and applied for the job as his executive assistant. She could have worked as a model if she hadn't been able to break in as a designer. She looked amazing in all the lingerie she wore.

The image of her standing in his office in just that black bra and G-string held together with bows flashed through his mind again. Hell, that image had never really left his mind. She was so damn sexy. And much too distracting...

He needed to find out if she really was the mole,

especially now with the guys putting pressure on him over getting involved with her. What if she wasn't?

Would she—could she—sue him for seducing her? Of course she'd seduced him first, though. Why?

Had she realized that he was onto her?

He pressed the intercom button on his phone.

"Yes?" Her voice filled his office, just like her scent and her image did.

"I'd like to see you..." In the flesh and not just in his mind. Due to the meeting with his partners, he hadn't seen her yet this morning. And there was a strange tightness in his chest.

She hesitated a long moment before replying with, "I have to finish a couple of things first."

"Are you stalling?" Maybe she didn't want to see him as badly as he wanted—as he needed—to see her.

She sighed. "No. I was distracted this morning with a visit."

Who had come to see her?

"Who was your visitor?" he asked. In the two years she'd worked for him, he couldn't remember anyone ever coming by to see her.

From what she'd said, her family didn't approve of her moving to the city. So they probably never visited. What about friends? He'd never met any of them. But then it wasn't as if they were dating or anything.

After another long pause, she replied, "Your partners."

He suppressed a groan. Why hadn't they trusted him to handle this—to handle her—on his own? After all, he was the managing partner. And that was because Street Legal had been his idea. He'd come up with the plan back when they'd all been living on the streets:

Go to college.

Get their law degrees.

Start their own practice.

They should have trusted that he would do whatever necessary to protect that practice. Of course doing Bette Monroe was no hardship.

"Bette, I need you in here right now." As he said it, a chill chased down his spine. He really did need her.

She sighed again, a sigh of frustration, and murmured, "I'm coming."

"Not yet," he said, then promised, "but you will be."

"Simon!" She admonished him, but there was amusement in her voice. And it certainly wasn't long before his door opened and she hurried inside.

Did she need him as much as he needed her?

He damn well hoped so—because he didn't like this feeling, as if the balance of power had shifted in her favor. As if he needed her more…

That wasn't the case, he assured himself. He needed the truth. He needed to know if she was, indeed, the mole.

"What did you want?" she asked as she strode over to his desk, her heels clicking against the hardwood floor. She wore another of her pencil-slim skirts with another cardigan. The skirt was gray, the sweater a deep purple. He wondered more what she wore beneath them.

"You," he said. "I want you."

Her lips curved into a smile. "Simon..."

But she didn't protest. Instead, she walked around his desk and pushed back his chair. And he knew she wanted him just as badly as he wanted her.

Instead of unbuttoning her cardigan or wriggling out of her skirt, she reached for the zipper on his pants as she dropped to her knees in front of him.

His cock swelled and pulsated, begging for the release he knew she could—and would—give him. But he couldn't let her seduce him again. He had to be the seducer.

This time he wanted more than sex from her. He wanted the truth. He didn't believe she was really falling for him. If he demanded it, would she tell him everything? Would she finally answer his questions and be completely honest with him?

Was she capable of complete honesty, though?

So few people really were.

He caught her hand before she could tug down his zipper and held it in his for a long moment. She stared up at him, her dark eyes wide with surprise.

"I thought that's why you called me in here."

"Then why didn't you come running?" he asked. "If you're really falling for me?"

She smiled her siren's smile at him. "Sometimes it's more satisfying when we have to wait."

Like the day they arrived at the office and had to get out of the car. That had been one long damn day.

He shook his head. "I'm not a patient man, Bette."

"I'm patient," she said. "I waited two years for you to notice me."

Had she really, though?

He pulled off the glasses she wore and dropped them onto his desk. Then he reached for the pins in her thick, luxurious hair, letting the silken tresses fall down around her shoulders.

"Or did you spend two years trying to make certain I wouldn't notice you?" he asked.

And that smile curved her lips even more.

She was the most challenging woman he'd ever met. How hadn't he noticed that about her? He'd seen her beauty despite her attempts to disguise it. But he'd never realized how clever and conniving she could be.

"Some men like the librarian look," she said.

He nodded in agreement. "I am some men," he admitted. Then he reached for the buttons on her cardigan, flicking them open to reveal the lacy camisole she wore beneath. It must have been designed by the same maddening person who designed her lingerie because there were little bows on the pink lace. "I also am the some men who love lingerie."

Her smile widened even more. "You love my lingerie?"

His breath shuddered out in appreciation. "Oh, yeah." But after pushing the cardigan from her shoulders, he reached for the bow that held up her camisole in the back. After he tugged it loose, it slipped down and revealed her naked breasts. "But I love your body even more."

Love. The word felt strange on his tongue. But in this case it wasn't a con. He really did love her body. It wouldn't betray him like her clever mind or her greedy heart might.

He flicked a fingertip over her nipple and it tightened in reaction. Her body could keep no secrets from him. He knew exactly what pleased it.

What pleased *her*...

He spent a long time on her breasts. Massaging the fullness of them, teasing the tight nipples. She moaned and wriggled and arched and finally she gasped as she came—just from his playing with her breasts.

He'd never known a woman as responsive as she was, as passionate. Or as generous.

She kept trying to undress him, reaching for the buttons on his shirt or the tab of his zipper. But he caught her wrists and locked them together in one of his hands, holding her back.

Then he moved his other hand between her legs. He stroked over the lace covering her mound. That was all he did, stroke his fingers over and over across the mound and over her clit. And she came again, nearly sobbing his name.

"What are you doing to me?" she asked. "Why?"

"You act like I'm punishing you," he said with a slight grin.

"Are you?" she asked.

If she was the mole, he would punish her. But this wasn't punishment. "This is pleasure, Bette. Don't you know the difference?"

"Pleasure is better if it's shared," she told him. And she tugged her wrists free of his grasp. Then she attacked the buttons of his shirt and the zipper on his pants.

After stripping off his clothes, she rolled a condom onto him. He wasn't sure if she'd found the condom in his pants or if she'd brought it with her. But he didn't care. He didn't care about anything but feeling the pleasure she'd promised him—that he knew she could deliver.

His body was wound so tight that he didn't move. He stayed in his office chair, his bare ass against the supple leather. And she straddled him.

As she guided his cock inside her, she settled onto his lap and released a shaky breath. He sank so deeply into her this way, was joined more completely with her than he had ever been. She must have felt it, too.

Her brown eyes widened in shock and pleasure. "You feel so damn good…"

He shook his head. "Are preachers' daughters supposed to swear?"

"I do a lot of things preachers' daughters aren't supposed to do," she told him. "Like you..." Then she kissed him, her tongue sliding between his lips like he slid into her body.

He arched his hips, thrusting up as she moved with him. Their mouths mated like their bodies—in a frantic rhythm. The chair creaked and rocked and threatened to break beneath the weight of their bodies and the crazy motion of them. But Simon only bought the best, so it held up.

And he tried to hold on...to his control. He tried to wait. But she kept rocking and bouncing and driving him out of his mind.

The tension wound so tightly in his body he felt that he might break before the chair. Like he might just snap...

She cried out and tensed as her inner muscles convulsed and clutched at his cock. Then heat rushed over him. She was coming. He tried to hold off, tried to give her more orgasms. But then his body stilled as his control exploded. And he came, her name on his lips.

He'd tried to seduce her. But just like every time before, she wound up seducing him. She was so damn hot. So damn sexy...

"Oh, Simon," she murmured as she settled her head against his shoulder. "You really are trying to make me love you."

That had been the new twist in his plan. But just like the seduction, he had to make sure it went according to plan. That she was the one who actually fell for him. Not the other way around...

Bette could have used Simon's private bathroom. But after the encounter she'd just had with him, she needed some space. Some perspective and some cold water splashed on her face. When she'd said what she had to him...

It hadn't been premeditated. It had just slipped out. Like she'd meant it.

But she couldn't mean it.

No. She'd just spent too much time too close to the sun, to the heat and passion that was Simon. So she needed to cool off. She rushed into the staff bathroom and headed toward the sink.

The doors of two of the stalls were closed, and the occupants spoke to each other. She shuddered in disgust. Apparently, she was in some ways still the repressed preacher's daughter.

"So how long do you think it's been going on?" the occupant of one stall asked the other. "The entire two years she's worked for him?"

The other woman laughed. "I don't think so. How could she have stayed when he was dating all those other women, too?"

"Maybe she has no pride."

Oh, my God. They were talking about her. She

stiffened with the very pride they didn't think she possessed.

"He's Simon Kramer," the first woman said with a lustful sigh. "For him I would have no pride, either."

"She's so damn lucky," the other agreed with a lustful sigh of her own. "I would love to work for and under him."

Bette had no idea who the women were, but if they were so eager to work for Simon, why hadn't they applied for her job?

"Well, you know he'll be done with her someday, just like he's been with all his other women. Maybe she'll summon some pride and quit then, and her job will open up."

"I can only hope."

A toilet flushed. Then another.

Bette could have turned on her heel and hurried out of the room. But despite what they thought, she had too much pride to run from the gossipy women. As the stall doors swung open and they stepped out, she stared at both of them.

One gave a nervous laugh and remarked, "We didn't realize you'd come in."

And she wondered about that. Even growing up in a small town in the generally friendly Midwest, she'd known mean girls. While these women hadn't been girls for a while—they were easily ten years older than her twenty-eight—they could still be mean. And they were obviously gossipy.

She shrugged. "I'm sure it wouldn't have stopped you if you had."

The woman's eyes widened at her boldness. "Well, of course we wouldn't—"

"What do you expect?" the other interrupted. "You're screwing your boss."

"He won't be my boss much longer." Just a little over four days. It didn't matter to her that Simon hadn't posted her position. She wasn't staying beyond the two weeks even if he hadn't replaced her.

One of the women tilted her head and gave Bette a fake sympathetic smile. "Oh, he's already dumped you."

Bette laughed. "I gave my notice before we even started..."

What?

They weren't dating. They had only shared that one meal together. They'd never attended a show or a movie together. No. They weren't dating.

They were just having sex and lots of it.

But she was fine with that. Dating would make it real. And it wasn't real. It was just a dream, a very real dream. But that dream needed to end soon or it was bound to become a nightmare.

She was afraid—very afraid—that she wasn't conning him anymore with her warnings that she was going to fall in love with him.

She was conning herself to think that she wasn't.

CHAPTER TEN

THE DOOR TO Simon's office opened with such force that it slammed against the wall. He glanced up from his desk in surprise and was even more surprised when he saw Bette standing in the doorway. Her face was flushed, and her eyes were bright with anger.

He'd never seen her like this. But as he did with everything about her, he found it incredibly sexy. He was also concerned. "What's wrong?"

Just as she'd slammed the door open, she slammed it closed and strode over to his desk. "I wondered why you hadn't been interviewing replacements for me."

Because he didn't think anyone could replace her. He'd never known anyone like Bette Monroe before. Not that he knew her even now. She was an enigma to him. A puzzle he had yet to find all the pieces to, like the proof of whether or not she was the mole.

But even if she was, he wasn't in any hurry to replace her. He would take his time screening applicants from now on and make sure he knew everything about them before he hired them. Because he'd had no idea when he'd hired Bette how passionate she was or what she wore beneath her conservative clothes.

If he'd known, he certainly wouldn't have waited two years to seduce her.

"But I didn't realize that you hadn't even posted my job yet," she continued.

He leaned back in his chair, the chair on which they'd just had sex. "For some reason I don't think you're really going to leave."

"Yes, I am!" she exclaimed. "I will only be here four more days."

A pang struck his heart. Was it possible? Would she really be gone that soon? That pang, that felt almost like panic, was only because he hadn't discovered the evidence against her. That had to be what it was. It couldn't be that he was upset that his time with her was coming to an end.

Two weeks was about the longest any of his relationships ever lasted anyway. Usually, he grew bored before then, or the woman started making demands that he wouldn't ever be prepared to meet. Like a commitment...

And he always got too bored to commit to anyone. He'd always be looking for the next challenge, just like he had his entire life.

Maybe that was why he hadn't grown bored with Bette yet. She challenged him like no one else ever had.

"You should already be interviewing candidates for your new assistant," she told him.

"I thought you'd be devastated if I tried to replace you," he said, "what with you falling in love with me and all."

She'd never actually said that she loved him, but she'd claimed that she was falling for him. But every time she'd told him that, she'd issued the statement like it was a threat.

And she'd had that little glimmer of mischief in her eyes that had told him she was up to something. Except for that last time, just moments ago when she laid her head on his chest...

Then she had seemed almost sincere. But maybe she'd just gotten better at the lie. Like his father used to say, a lie well told and stuck to was just as good as the truth.

Her face flushed now with embarrassment. And he knew that, just as he'd suspected, she'd been lying to him.

"What?" He arched a brow. "You're not in love with me?"

She didn't say anything. She just sighed. "I guess I might as well come clean with you now."

"What?" he repeated, and this time he was astounded. "You're going to tell me the truth?"

Would it be this easy? While she hadn't fallen in love with him, maybe she'd enjoyed their time together enough that she was feeling guilty over her betrayal.

"Please, Bette," he implored her. "Be honest with me."

Her face flushed a darker shade of red and she wouldn't meet his gaze. "You're going to get mad at me."

And his heart plummeted in his chest. She was the mole. While he should be relieved to know his suspicions were right, he was disappointed. Hell, he was more than disappointed.

He was devastated. For the first time in his life, he had actually wanted to be wrong.

Not that he'd gotten attached to her or anything. But at least he wouldn't have been conned when he'd hired her, when he'd trusted her.

Apparently, that was not the case.

Apparently, he never should have trusted her.

Bette studied his face, waiting for him to assure her that he wouldn't get mad at her. But he didn't. Instead, he just looked very tense, his jaw tightly clenched.

But she shouldn't care if he got mad. In fact, maybe that would be the best way to get him to release her four days early from serving out the rest of her two weeks. Or maybe it would at least get him to post her job.

She drew in a deep breath and admitted, "I've been playing you."

He released a sharp breath as if she'd punched him.

But he nodded and said, "That's what I thought." He cursed and admitted, "I'd just hoped I was wrong."

"That night I undressed in the office." Heat rushed from her face throughout the rest of her body as she thought of that night, of how she'd taken off her glasses and taken down her hair...

She should have stopped there. But then she never would have known what sex with Simon Kramer was like and why all those other women had been so desperate for it to never stop. She didn't want to become that desperate, though.

So she had to make sure there was an end in sight for them. For the sex and the job.

"I was playing you," she said.

His brow furrowed. "You didn't really want to have sex?"

"I—I had always wondered what it would be like to be with you," she admitted. "I just didn't have this undying attraction to you that I'd said I had."

He stood up now and walked around his desk. He didn't reach for her, though. In fact, he leaned back against the front of his desk and crossed his arms over his chest. "You're not attracted to me?"

She snorted with self-derision. "I'm not a liar. Of course I'm attracted, but I'm not in love with you." At least she didn't think she was.

Of course she wasn't...

"I just wanted you to think that I was falling for you," she said.

"But why?"

"So you wouldn't make me work out the two-week notice," she said.

He shook his head as if he was having trouble following her—which was strange since she'd figured he was onto her this entire time. "How would that make me release you from the terms of your employment contract?"

She snorted again but this time in derision of him. "I've worked for you for two years," she reminded him. "I see how you treat women."

His face flushed now, his skin getting a little ruddy. "What do you mean?"

"As soon as they profess any feelings for you, you dump them," she said.

"You think that makes me heartless?" he asked.

She'd thought once that it had but now she understood. "It's probably the nicest thing you can do," she said. "If you're not able to return their feelings, it's better to break it off before they fall any harder."

"You sound as if you're speaking from experience," he mused.

She shrugged and admitted, "I've never been in love." She'd been too focused on fashion—on her designs.

"But you've had men fall for you?"

She shrugged again. There had been boys in school who'd professed love. She figured they'd just been trying to get her to have sex with them. She hadn't really believed they'd loved her—not when they hadn't really known her. But then they hadn't cared about her goals and aspirations. They'd cared only about their own. And if she'd fallen for them, she would have gotten sucked into their lives instead of living her own. Just like her mom and sister had and countless other women she'd known.

"I don't know," she said, willing to give those old boyfriends the benefit of the doubt. "Who knows if another person's feelings are real?"

He chuckled. "Apparently, I don't."

"You didn't really think I was falling for you," she said. "Or you would have cut me loose last week."

He grinned. "Why would I have done that again?"

"You can't stand clingy women," she said. "So I was trying to act clingy."

"Hmm, I guess I didn't see the clinginess."

"We've been spending so much time together," she reminded him. "More time than you've spent with any other woman."

"That's because we work together," he said.

"We haven't been working the whole time," she reminded him. And she gestured around his office at the couch and the chair and the desk and the conference table.

They'd had sex on every surface in his office. And on every surface in hers.

"You've been working me," he said. "Why didn't you want to work out the two weeks? Did you tell your new employer you'd start sooner?"

She shook her head. She was already working for them. She'd been working for them for years as a freelance design assistant. Between Street Legal and fashion, all she'd done was work. Maybe that was why sex with Simon was so amazing.

Because she'd denied herself too long.

"Maybe I felt like you with all those women you refused to see again after you broke up with them," she told him. "Once I gave my notice, I didn't want to have to keep coming back here for two more weeks."

"Why not?" he asked.

"I didn't want to keep seeing you." And she knew that was probably as much her reason as wanting to start working only on her new line. Despite everything, she knew that she would miss working with Simon. He had the same passion for his job that she had for fashion.

But it wasn't just her designs that she had a passion for anymore. It was Simon, too.

He pressed a hand over his heart and said, "Ouch. Guess that's karma for me."

"You've broken a lot of hearts," she reminded him. And she'd mopped up some of those tears for him. She hoped she wouldn't wind up mopping up her own before the week was out. "That's why I know better than to fall for you, because I know you too well."

He arched a brow. "That sounds like a challenge."

She shook her head. "No, not at all."

But he was already reaching for her. "I'll make you clingy," he warned her as he lowered his head to hers. Despite the grin curving his lips, he kissed her deeply. And as he kissed her, sliding his tongue in and out of her mouth, he touched her.

He ran his hands over her breasts, but he didn't undress her. He didn't need to. She could feel the heat of his touch through her clothes, and her nipples tightened. She moaned. Then he moved his hands lower, over her hips and ass.

She arched her hips against him, feeling his erection through her clothes and his. But it wasn't enough. She wanted him inside her.

Then he lifted her, and just as he'd promised, she was clinging to him. He shoved up her skirt and pulled her panties aside, and somehow his zipper was down and he'd rolled on a condom. Then he was inside her, thrusting deep. And she clung to him, her arms and legs wrapped tightly around him. She clung as he drove her up and out of her mind with pleasure.

He felt so good. His cock so long and hard. As he continued to thrust, the tension wound tightly inside her. She ached for release, and finally, an orgasm slammed through her, making her body shudder with the explosive power of the release. He caught her cry of pleasure in his mouth as he continued to kiss her. And he didn't stop thrusting his hips, didn't stop driving as deeply as only he could, until she came again and again.

Her muscles quivered and she could barely hold on, her body was so limp with pleasure. Then finally, a deep groan ripped from his throat and he came, too. His legs shook slightly beneath their combined

weights, and he leaned his forehead, damp with per-
spiration, against hers.

Staring deeply into her eyes, he said, "For some
reason I don't mind when you're clingy, Bette Monroe."

She minded. And she was scared to death that she
really might fall for him.

CHAPTER ELEVEN

SHE WAS GONE. Simon knew it the moment he stepped out of the elevator. Of course he shouldn't have been surprised; it was well after five. Everyone else was gone, too, except maybe for Stone.

His office was far enough down the hall that Simon couldn't see if a light was burning under his door. But his own office was dark. He headed toward it anyway. Since he was just returning from a dinner meeting with a client, he had some notes to drop off on his desk.

He pushed open the door and uttered a sigh of disappointment when he confirmed it was empty. It would have been nice had Bette been waiting for him wearing only her naughty lingerie. But just as he'd suspected when he'd stepped off the elevator, she was gone for the night.

If she'd been there, he would have felt her presence in the tingling of his skin and quickening of his pulse. When she was around, he was always aware of her and the attraction that sizzled between them.

But attraction was all it was. She'd confirmed that

this afternoon when she'd confessed that she wasn't falling for him, that it had all just been a con.

Was that the only one she'd run on him? Or was there another one—a far more dangerous one—at least to the practice and to his pride?

The guys didn't understand how a con worked. That she would leave even though she was making money off them. She'd do that if she was as smart as he'd known she was. Quit before you get caught— that was what had kept him out of prison while he'd been growing up.

His father hadn't been able to say the same.

The other part of a good con was to disarm the mark's suspicions with a confession—but only to confess something innocuous, like her pretending to fall for him. That way the mark wouldn't suspect there were any more secrets.

He suspected Bette Monroe had many, many more secrets than what she'd confessed. And he intended to learn them all. But when he set his briefcase onto his desk, he found an envelope sitting on his keyboard addressed to him. He immediately recognized the artistic handwriting as Bette's. She'd already turned in her letter of resignation. What was this?

After today he knew it wasn't a love letter. She didn't love him, had laughed at the possibility of ever falling for him.

Because she had someone else? Someone who was willing to support her? He could. Hell, he would if she asked. He doubted that was what this letter was about, either.

His hand shaking slightly, he tore open the envelope and pulled out the piece of paper. It wasn't a letter at all. It was a job description—her job description. And at the bottom of the list of her duties was another, but it was his.

You need to post my position ASAP.

And he knew she wasn't staying. What the hell had happened to him? He used to be such a good con artist. He hadn't met a woman who he hadn't been able to seduce into doing what he wanted. But while Bette had sex with him, she wasn't malleable. She wasn't staying.

And she wasn't revealing any of her secrets.

He needed to turn up the seduction. Despite her claim of knowing him too well to fall for him, he had to make her love him. That was the only way he suspected he would get the truth out of her.

But he was beginning to worry that wasn't what he really wanted from Bette Monroe. He wanted even more than the truth.

Did he want her love?

Despite all the women who'd claimed to feel that way about him, he'd never really believed it, just as Bette had seemed to doubt the profession of love she'd had. Was it because—like him—he'd felt like none of those women had known him well enough to love him?

Only his friends knew him well enough to love him.

But if he wanted Bette's love, he would have to let her know him. Really know him. Not just what she thought she knew about him. After working for him for two years, she probably already knew him better than most. And then he'd told her more than he had anyone else.

Damn.

Who was conning whom?

Bette Monroe was far more dangerous than he'd thought. Even if she was the mole, she was only a danger to the firm. Now she had become a danger to him…

Bette flinched as she felt a twinge of guilt. Maybe she should have waited for Simon to return to the office before she left. But he hadn't asked her to stay. Maybe he had assumed that she would.

But she'd finished her work. Most important, she'd listed the duties for her job description. He needed to know that no matter how much charm he turned on her, she wasn't staying. These two weeks were already cutting in to valuable time that she needed to come up with more designs.

Pride coursed through her. She'd accomplished what she'd always dreamed of doing. She had her own line and for the premier retailer of lingerie worldwide. They loved her creativity and innovation.

She could not disappoint them or herself. She

couldn't sacrifice her dream for a man. She had too many friends who had. Her mother and sister had done that and now lived dull lives of quiet resentment. She had no intention of ever winding up like them.

She didn't need a man.

But she wanted one...

An emptiness stretched inside her, an emptiness she was never aware of until she had started having sex with Simon, until he'd filled her.

Completed her.

She shook her head and laughed at herself. While she loved designing lingerie, she was not some hopeless romantic. She didn't need a man to complete her. She didn't need Simon.

She needed to focus on her designs. So she returned her attention to the sketch pad lying across her bed. Tightening her fingers around her pen, she swept it across the page as she designed a corset with, of course, her signature bow. Bette's Beguiling Bows—that was the name of her line. She put the bow at the bottom, though, so it would sit atop her ass, where Simon loved her bows. Even when she had her clothes on, he skimmed his fingers over her skirt until he found it.

What would he think of this design?

She couldn't wait to sew up a prototype to get his opinion. But that would take a couple of days and... she only had four before she left Street Legal. That didn't necessarily mean that their relationship would have to end. But then it wasn't really a relationship.

She wasn't sure what the hell it was.

And she didn't think he knew, either.

Her doorbell rang, and her pen shot across the page as her heart leaped. It could have been a friend. She'd shared her new address, with the ones who hadn't already known it, when they'd called to complain about being MIA the past week. She'd explained that she needed to finish up things at work before she could leave. But what she needed to finish the most at work was whatever this thing with Simon was.

No. They could not continue seeing each other once she left. She would be too busy. And he was too…Simon. He would grow bored soon, if he hadn't already.

The doorbell rang again, as if someone was leaning against the button. And she knew that he hadn't grown bored yet. Smiling, she headed toward the door. A quick glance out the peephole confirmed her suspicions regarding the identity of her visitor.

It wasn't one of her girlfriends.

Her pulse quickened, and her skin tingled. As she opened the door, she asked the question she'd wondered the last time he'd shown up at her apartment, "How do you keep getting past security?"

"I know the doorman," he said, his face flushing slightly as he looked away.

"You dated someone in the building," she guessed.

He nodded.

"A model?"

A model had recommended the building to her. Her friend Muriel also had an apartment in it.

He nodded again. And his face grew a little redder. But she realized he wasn't embarrassed when he held out a crumpled-up piece of paper to her. He was mad.

She sighed and stepped back as he strode into her apartment. "I already know you crumpled up my resignation," she reminded him. "It still doesn't change the fact that I'm leaving."

"You made that clear when you left this on my desk," he said.

And she saw what the paper was. "Ah, my job description," she said. "I figured that would help you when you post the job, which you should have done last week."

"Bette…"

"Unless you intend to just hire someone through a temp agency," she continued. "That's your prerogative."

"Yes, it is," he said. "It's my business. Isn't that what you keep saying to me?"

She smiled at his grumpiness.

"This isn't funny," he said.

"You really aren't used to it, are you?" she asked. "Your charm not getting you your way."

He tensed and stared down at her as if he'd just realized that was the case. "It's not exactly like you're immune to me," he said as he stepped closer to her. And as if he'd once again taken her words as a challenge, he touched her, sliding his thumb across the fullness of her bottom lip.

Her breath escaped in a gasp as desire raced through her. But he sighed wistfully, as well.

"I'm not immune to you, either," he said. "You make me forget..."

"What?" she asked.

But he just shook his head.

"To post my job?" she teased.

"How can I forget that?" he asked. "When you keep nagging me about it?"

She took the crumpled-up piece of paper from his hand. "You didn't like my job description?"

"I think some things are missing," he said.

"Like what?"

He slid his hands over her ass. "Like 'must look good in a tight skirt.'"

She'd been so eager to start working on her designs that she hadn't changed yet. She'd only taken off her cardigan. The camisole she wore beneath it was silk and so thin that it was evident that her nipples had tightened. They pushed against the fabric as his fingers traced the bow on her underwear.

"And 'must wear lingerie under those tight skirts.'"

She was on board with that. She needed to sell out her line to impress the retailer and extend her contract with them. "Might be kind of hard for a man to find skirts and corsets big enough."

He chuckled and lowered his head to hers, pressing a quick kiss against her lips. "I never knew how funny you are, Bette Monroe," he said.

"Yeah, I'm quitting Street Legal to devote myself full-time to my stand-up act," she said.

He chuckled again but then sighed. "Hell, maybe you are."

It would probably be more believable to most than finding out she was a lingerie designer.

"I feel like I barely know you at all."

It was true. He barely did. But she'd done that to protect herself. She didn't want to get too close to him. She didn't want to really fall for him.

"What are you going to do once you quit?"

She tensed.

And his grumpiness returned as, his voice gruff with irritation, he asked, "How can that still be none of my business?"

"What do you think has changed?" she asked.

"I've seen you naked."

She smiled and shook her head.

"I haven't?" he asked with an arched brow. "Do you have a body double I've been having sex with, then?"

She laughed and said, "You've definitely seen me without my clothes. But you haven't really seen me naked." Telling him about the hopes and dreams she had worked so hard to pursue would have truly been the way she would have lain herself bare to him. And she wasn't ready to do that with someone she couldn't trust.

His brow furrowed as if he was confused.

So she added, "I haven't seen you naked, either. Not really. I don't know much more about you than Allison McCann has put out in the press releases for Street Legal."

He cocked his head and studied her face, skepticism on his handsome one. "Really? After working for me for two years…"

"I know how you've been the past two years," she said. "About how hard you work…" She smiled to soften her next words. "How hard you play…"

Because the conversation was getting so serious between them, she wanted to play now. She was far more comfortable with that than with the conversation heading where it was—into very personal and private matters of hearts and souls.

She wasn't ready to let him see either her heart or her soul. Not now—not when they had so little time left to be together and not when she was beginning to feel so damn vulnerable with him.

She stepped closer to him until her body pressed against his. Arching her hips into his, into the erection straining against the fly of his suit pants, she teased, "I love how *hard* you play…"

He narrowed his eyes as if he was completely aware that she was trying to distract him and he wondered why. But he couldn't resist her any easier than she could resist him. Those narrowed eyes darkened as his pupils dilated, and his chest began to rise and fall as his breathing grew faster and shallower.

Her pulse quickened even more than it had when he rang the bell. He excited her so damn much with his touch and his kiss.

But he didn't touch or kiss her. He just continued to stare at her. And she knew she wasn't the only one who was afraid of being seen naked—truly naked. Simon wasn't any more comfortable about laying himself bare to her.

She'd once thought that he didn't have a heart or a soul. But now she knew he had them. He just hid them to protect them, like she did.

And knowing that about him, knowing that they had something in common, scared her even more. She could not fall in love with Simon Kramer.

CHAPTER TWELVE

WHAT THE HELL did she do to him? With her, he had no control. He couldn't resist her; he couldn't do anything but want her.

He swung her up in his arms and carried her toward the room that had to be her bedroom. But she caught the jamb before he could carry her over the threshold.

"Put me down," she told him.

"What—why?" Had she changed her mind? That wasn't like her. She didn't have much more control than he did once they started kissing.

Touching…

"I—I have to put something away first," she said. She wriggled down from his arms and rushed into the bedroom.

Before he could follow her inside, she closed the door on his face. As if that wasn't bad enough, he heard a lock click, as well.

She really did not want him inside her bedroom. The last time he'd been in her apartment, he hadn't gotten beyond the couch in the living room where they'd had sex. Tonight he'd wanted to be in her bed nearly as badly as he wanted to be inside her.

But now he wondered if he would be allowed in either? Had she locked herself inside for the night? Did she want him to leave?

Stunned, he could only stand there for several long moments. What the hell was going on in there? What was she doing? He lifted his hand to knock, but before his fist could strike the white-painted wood, the door opened.

She reached for his hand and tugged him inside the room with her. Looking over her head, he peered around the space. Like the living room, the floors were dark hardwood—the plaster ceilings high. The exterior wall was brick with a tall window while the other walls were painted a dreamy blue. The bed, a fluffy-looking queen-size one, shared the space with a library table that had been converted to a desk. If she'd taken any records from the office, they were probably stashed in that desk.

"Should I check the closet?" he asked. "Did you push a lover in there?"

She laughed. "No. I was getting this out of the closet." She stepped back and twirled around to show off the negligee she wore. It wasn't as long as the one she'd had on the first day he'd come to her apartment. This one barely covered her luscious ass.

Like all her other outfits, it had a bow on it— this one on the front—at the top of the satin ribbon that crisscrossed the bodice, binding it together. The pale blue fabric was a wispy lace through which her nipples showed.

He groaned. "Damn, woman, how much of this stuff do you own?"

And who had bought it for her? Had she bought it for herself? Or had a lover picked out the lingerie for her to wear for him?

Something flashed through him—something he hadn't felt since he was a kid—envying kids who'd had a mom and a dad and a house, who hadn't had to con people for money for food and clothes.

How he'd hated those kids, hated that they'd taken for granted what he'd always wished he had.

Her brow puckered as she stared up at him; she must have caught the expression on his face. "Don't you like it?"

He automatically reached for the bow, running his fingers over the satin ribbon. "I love it," he said. "I love it all..." Most of all, he loved her body, the sweet curves of it, the soft skin.

The heat and the passion that burned him when he slid inside her, when he slid home. Desperate for her, he tugged the bow loose so the negligee dropped from her body. Then he pushed her back onto the bed.

He'd never felt this way, never felt so desperate to claim someone as his. Hell, he'd never wanted to claim anyone as his—until Bette.

He moved his hands and lips over her body, spreading his kiss and caress as if he were branding her as his. He had never felt possessive of another human being before. Had never felt this madness in his blood and his fiercely pounding heart.

Her heart pounded just as fast and furiously beneath his palm that cupped her breast. She was just as excited as he was, her chest heaving as she panted for breath.

He'd never had anyone match his passion the way Bette did. He didn't have to make sure she was ready for him. He knew she already was. And of course when he stroked his fingers over her mound, he found her hot and ready. And a pulse beat there for him, in her clit.

Her breath shuddered out as she arched off the bed. "Simon…"

She needed him just as badly as he needed her. But with her, he wanted to make sure she got as much pleasure as he did. So he moved down her body. And he slid his tongue over her clit, back and forth.

She whimpered and shifted against the bed. Her hands clutched his shoulder and then his hair. "Simon!"

He thrust his fingers inside her. And she came.

His vision blurred as his desire intensified to insanity. He undressed in such a frenzy that a button popped off. Then he tore open a condom packet and sheathed himself before sliding inside her.

She was so hot. So wet. So ready…

She moved beneath him and around him. They rolled across the sheets, tangling them, tearing them from the bed. Passion burned between them. They clutched at each other. Despite her release, she was desperate again, desperate for more pleasure. He made sure she got it, making her come again and again before he finally let himself come.

Then he dropped limply onto her body, struggling to breathe again as his heart finally began to slow its frantic beating. He raised his head from her breast and stared up at her in wonder. "What the hell do you do to me?"

She just shook her head. She either didn't know or couldn't speak. So he didn't think she'd be able to move, either. But after cleaning up in the bathroom, he strode back into her bedroom, and she wasn't there.

Where the hell had she gone?

"Bette?"

She stepped out of the other door, the one to the walk-in closet. But she was wearing only the robe that had been lying across the foot of the bed. So why had she gone back inside there?

Was she hiding something in there? Or in the desk? She glanced at that, too, as if checking to make sure she'd left nothing out. But then she grabbed up his shirt from the bedroom floor and held it out to him.

"Trying to get rid of me?" he asked.

"Uh, no," she stammered, but her eyes widened in surprise. "You don't want to stay, though."

She must have heard that rule of his, how he never spent the night with anyone. If he wanted a chance to search her closet and that desk, he was going to need to make an exception to that rule. So she wouldn't catch him snooping again, like she nearly had last time, he had to wait until after she fell asleep.

"You are trying to get rid of me," he said, and the hurt he allowed in his voice wasn't entirely feigned. "I really should check to see who you have stashed in that closet."

"Nobody," she replied quickly, almost too quickly.

He doubted any man could have hidden in there while they'd had sex. Even if he was married, Simon damn well wouldn't have done it. He would have taken apart the guy who dared to touch her while he was seeing her.

"You really aren't seeing anyone else?" he asked.

"No," she said. "I told you I don't have time for dating right now."

"What are we doing, then?" he asked.

"We're not dating," she said. "That's why it would be weird for you to stay."

He'd had women beg him to spend the night in their beds. But this one—the one with whom he actually wanted to spend the night—seemed almost on the verge of begging him to leave. He reached for her, closing his arms around her shoulders to draw her close to his chest. "How 'bout I just stay until I recover enough for us to do that again?"

She rubbed her hips against his. "I think you're recovered enough."

He chuckled. He was. Just being close to her made

him hard as hell. "Not quite yet." He tugged her toward the bed, pulled back the tangled blankets and pulled her down onto the mattress with him.

"You really want to stay?" she asked.

"Just for a little while," he lied. He didn't know how long he'd have to stay for her to fall asleep.

She settled her head against his shoulder. "What do you want to do until you recover?" she asked.

"Talk."

She tensed.

"Don't worry," he told her. "I'll talk. You can just listen."

She must have been intrigued enough that she moved her hand to his chest, and her fingers began to stroke the skin over his heart. Did she feel how hard it was beating yet for her?

"I will post your job," he promised her.

She released a shaky sigh but he didn't know if it was of relief or disappointment.

"Do you want me to add the tight skirts and lingerie into the job description?" she asked.

He shook his head. "No. It would be hard for a guy to find and I probably would be better off with a male assistant. I'd be less distracted—" he moved his hand down her back to the curve of her hip and ass "—because you sure as hell distracted me the past two years."

She snorted in disbelief.

"You did," he insisted. "I couldn't stop staring at your ass..."

A giggle slipped through her lips. Then she suggested, "Maybe Miguel has a friend. Another reformed gang member."

"Too damn few of his friends are even alive yet, let alone reformed like he is," he said.

"How long have you known Miguel?" she asked.

"A hell of a lot longer than two years," he said. "I knew him from when I lived on the streets."

"Why were you living on the streets? Did you run away from home?" she asked.

And he was glad that she had, that she actually wanted to know something about him. Other women had pried for information about his life, about his past. Until now, Bette hadn't seemed to care. She hadn't wanted to get to know him.

But maybe if she did, she would open up to him, too. So he told her everything: about never knowing his mom, about his dad training him to con people before he'd hardly known how to walk or talk, about how the only way he'd been able to escape that life was to run away from his father.

"Didn't he try to find you?" she asked.

He shook his head.

She stroked her hand over his heart as if she was trying to soothe away the hurt. Miraculously, her touch seemed to do just that. It didn't bother him like it usually did when he talked about his father.

"It would have been hard for him to look for me," he said, "since shortly after I ran away, he got arrested."

She gasped, her breath brushing warmly across his skin.

He chuckled but without any humor. "Fortunately for me, he is still serving that sentence." If he wasn't, Simon would have suspected his father of somehow being the mole. Hell, even with him being in jail, it made more sense for him to be the mole than it did for Bette. But she had access; he didn't.

"Why is that fortunate?" she asked, her voice soft.

"Because he blamed me for his getting arrested," he said, then shrugged as if it didn't matter to him. But it did, and she must have known because she pressed her lips to his chest in a gentle kiss.

"Were you responsible?" she asked.

He'd never told anyone else this, but he felt compelled to tell her. "Yes. I turned him in, had some evidence."

"Did you do that just to get away from him?"

"He had to be stopped," Simon admitted. "He was conning people who couldn't afford it. I had to do some things...when I was living on the streets. But I made sure nobody got hurt. He didn't care."

Least of all about his son.

She must have heard what he left unsaid because she reached up and pressed a kiss to his lips and nuzzled her hair against his cheek. "Sounds like both our fathers disowned us."

He had never realized how much he had in common with Bette. She was an amazing woman, even if she was the damn mole. He hoped like hell that she wasn't, though.

He moved her hand from his chest to his groin. "Look, I'm recovered."

Her fingers closed around him, and she began to stroke him up and down. While she teased him with her touch, he reached for his pants and fished a condom from the pocket. Before he could sheathe himself, her mouth slid over his shaft—up and down. He nearly came then. But he wanted more.

He pushed her onto her back and feasted on her body, on her full breasts with the ultrasensitive nipples, on the curve of her hip, on her dimpled knee... then he moved between her legs. And he made certain she had recovered, as well.

Her fingers clutched his shoulders, and she dragged him up. Then she guided his cock inside her. They moved with less urgency this time. Taking their time with slow strokes and long kisses...

And when they came, they came together—shouting each other's names. Simon had never felt as connected to another person. Or as scared...

Bette felt connected to Simon in a way that had nothing to do with the physical. She felt connected to Simon emotionally. She'd seen him naked, truly naked. And she knew she should return the favor.

What he'd shared with her was far more personal than her career goals and dreams. What he'd shared with her...

Scared the hell out of her, not because of what he'd done or who he was. But because she was really beginning to fall for him. Panic coursed through her, like moments ago passion had, and she tensed.

She should tell him to leave, show him to the door. He'd already been here too long, too vividly. Now she would always imagine him here. It hadn't been bad when he'd been in just the living room. But now he'd been in the bedroom, in her bed. And like Goldilocks, he was still there. He must have fallen asleep, for his body—his beautiful body—was relaxed.

Instead of pounding on his chest to wake him up, she rested her head on it and curled up against his side. Sure, she had work to do. But she was tired. And she only had a few more days with him.

She would take a moment to enjoy just being with him. It wasn't as if he would actually spend the night. She was certain he would wake up and slip out before morning. If not much sooner.

The thought of him leaving relaxed her enough that she began to drift off to sleep. While her mind told her she wanted him gone, her body wrapped around his, holding him close. And she had to admit the truth.

She didn't want him to leave. Not just tonight but maybe ever.

That thought filled her with such terror that she jerked fully awake. She must have been asleep longer than she realized because he was gone. Her arms clutched nothing but the pillow that smelled yet like him. She should have been relieved that he'd left.

But a chill chased over her bare skin, raising goose bumps. She wasn't just cold, though. She was scared for a couple of reasons.

One—the disappointment that filled her over his slipping out. Sure, she'd suspected that he would. She'd even thought that would be a good thing. But she hadn't realized how good it would feel to actually sleep with him.

The second reason she was scared was because she heard a strange noise. The creak of floorboards and a weird scraping noise. It wasn't coming from the living room. So it wasn't Simon walking to the door. The noise emanated from her walk-in closet. She reached for her nightstand where she'd stashed her purse in the cabinet beneath the drawer, and she pulled out the canister of Mace she always carried.

With it clutched tightly, reassuringly, in her hand, she slipped into her robe, tied up the sash with her other hand and headed toward her closet door. She jerked it open and prepared to spray her intruder in the face…until she recognized him. Then she demanded to know, "What the hell are you doing?"

CHAPTER THIRTEEN

"WHAT THE HELL are you doing?" Bette demanded to know, and like he'd done the day he'd caught her in his office after hours, she had to ask him twice.

But he still didn't know how to answer her. Heat rushed to his face with embarrassment that he'd been caught snooping. He'd wanted to know what the hell she'd hidden in her closet. He'd noticed the clothes knocked askew on the bottom rack, and he'd reached behind to find what she'd stashed there.

It wasn't a man but a sketch pad. She had a portfolio full of them. Then he'd found the box of lingerie, which he was on his knees leaning over at the moment. And he understood that all those sexy outfits weren't gifts from a married lover or from any lover at all. Next to the box, he'd found a sewing machine and some reams of lace and silk. And he'd figured out what her big secret was and it wasn't selling any of Street Legal's secrets.

"Why didn't you just tell me?" he asked.

Her face flushed a bright red that nearly matched the color of the corset he held in his hands. "I don't have to tell you why I'm quitting," she said. "Even your employment contract states that."

"I know," he said. "You didn't have to tell me. But why wouldn't you?" Was she ashamed of what she did, because of her upbringing?

Her face flushed an even deeper shade of red. "You would have laughed."

That wasn't the reply he'd expected. "What? Why would you think that?"

"Boring Bette Monroe designing lingerie?" She uttered a short chuckle of her own, but it was full of bitterness. "Even I think that's funny."

He was more confused now than when he'd discovered her secret. "Why in the hell do you think you're boring?"

She snorted. "Come on, you thought that, too—the past two years."

His face heated a bit, and he had to admit that he had. But in his defense, he explained, "I was going off the way you pull your hair into such a tight bun and how you dress. I had no idea what you've been wearing under your clothes this entire time." He held up a handful of the lingerie. But even then he'd still been attracted to her; he'd seen her beauty no matter how hard she'd tried to hide it.

"Why do you dress that way?" he asked. "Why do you wear your hair that way? And the glasses, I don't even think you need them." He stepped closer to her. "What are you hiding from, Bette?"

She took the lingerie from his hand, but she wouldn't answer his question.

"Are you hiding from me?" he asked.

"Given your reputation, I thought it was a good idea to dress a little more conservatively than I used to," she said.

He flinched as a twinge of pain struck his heart. "You were afraid of me? Afraid that I'd force myself on you?"

Then he glanced down and saw that, in her hand not full of lingerie, she clutched a canister of Mace. He sighed. "I guess you are afraid of me."

"I thought you left," she said. "I didn't know who was in my closet. I can't believe you've been snooping through my stuff."

"I knew you were hiding something," he said. He'd thought she'd been hiding the evidence that she was the mole. But she wasn't. And he was so relieved that he laughed.

Anger flashed in her eyes. "See, I told you that you'd laugh at me!" She threw the lingerie at him and stomped back into the bedroom.

He rushed after her so quickly that he was still knocking G-strings off his shoulders as he joined her near the bed. "Guess I should be glad you didn't mace me."

"I almost did," she said. "You scared me."

"I'm sorry," he said.

"For scaring me or for snooping?" she challenged him.

"For scaring you," he admitted.

He'd hoped she would sleep through his search. And that he would be able to slip back into bed with her before she'd even noticed he'd left it. He hadn't wanted to. She'd felt so warm and soft and somehow comforting sleeping in his arms, her head against his chest.

"You're not sorry for snooping," she said with disgust.

He was unapologetic. "I had to find out the truth."

Her brow furrowed. "The truth about what?"

He couldn't tell her—not now. She was already mad at him. If he told her that he'd suspected her of selling secrets from Street Legal's case files, she would be furious, so furious that she would throw him out of her place and out of her life.

And he couldn't have that because then he couldn't have her. Now that he'd learned her secret, he wanted her even more.

"I already told you," he said. "I knew you were hiding something." He just hadn't realized that something was herself. "And you never answered me. You never told me why you were hiding from me. Are you afraid of me?"

Bette had never been as afraid of Simon as she was now. She was afraid that she was beginning to have feelings for him. She nearly laughed now over the irony of that. For days she'd wanted him to believe she was in love with him, so that he would cut her notice short. But now that she was actually falling, there was no way she wanted him to know.

She'd pretended to have feelings for him because she'd known it would horrify him. She didn't want to horrify him. But she did want to be honest with him just as he'd been honest with her.

"I'm afraid of becoming my mother or my sister," she said. "I don't want to get so into some guy that I forget who I am and what I want out of life."

He laughed again. But this time she didn't mind that he was laughing at her. "I think you know exactly who you are, Bette Monroe," he said. "It's the rest of the world you don't want to know you."

"My friends know me," she said.

"You don't dress in the cardigans and skirts around them?" he asked.

He probably hadn't seen much else in her closet.

"That's as much a habit from how I was raised as a way to hide," she said. "I had to dress conservatively when I was growing up."

"But you're all grown-up now," he said, and his blue eyes darkened with desire.

"I'm still mousy Bette in so many ways," she said.

And he laughed as if she'd told him the funniest joke he'd ever heard. Then he focused on her face and stopped. "You've got to be kidding," he said. "You can't really see yourself that way."

"That's how I saw myself for a lot of years," she admitted. "So it's a hard habit to break. Designing and wearing my lingerie makes me feel sexy, though."

"And beautiful," he added.

She smiled but shook her head. "And you told me you stopped conning people."

"I'm telling you the truth," he said. "You know the women I've dated."

She nodded. "Models. Actresses. That's why I know you're lying."

Anger flashed in his eyes now. He jerked her into his arms and tipped up her chin so she had to look into his face—his gorgeous face. "You, Bette Monroe, are a beautiful, sexy woman."

Maybe he was a hypnotist as well as a con artist because she was beginning to believe him, especially since he kept repeating those words between kisses.

His mouth nibbled at her lips. "Women pay to have lips like these," he said. "Full, silky, sexy..."

He tangled his fingers in her hair. "And this... It's real, no extensions." He pushed the robe from her body and skimmed his hand over her breasts. "Like these. You're real, Bette."

"I never knew that was sexy."

"The sexiest," he said.

And with the way he looked at her, she felt sexy, even without her lingerie. She felt sexy naked.

"And beautiful," he added.

He pushed her back onto the bed. And he touched and kissed her with an almost reverence, as if she was a work of art. She believed him.

She was no longer mousy Bette Monroe.

She was the siren he'd called her.

And she wanted him to feel what she was feeling. She wanted him to have feelings for her, too. So she pulled him down on top of her and pressed kisses to his chest and his shoulders and onto his washboard abs that rippled beneath her touch.

"Bette…"

"You're the beautiful one," she said.

Of course he didn't deny it. He couldn't not know how handsome he was. He'd undoubtedly used his looks when he'd conned those people with his father and with his friends when they'd all been struggling to survive on the streets.

And even though he'd claimed he'd stopped conning people, she worried that he was conning her now. Not into believing she was beautiful and sexy; she felt he was sincere about that. But she couldn't help but think he'd been trying to make her fall for him.

He joined their bodies again, driving his shaft inside her. She clung to him, riding him as he drove them both to insanity. The orgasm shuddered through her body, more powerful than any even he had given her before.

And she knew she was in trouble, that she was getting in deep…

CHAPTER FOURTEEN

"THIS ISN'T TUESDAY," Simon said as his partners stormed his office.

"Her last day is today," Trevor said. "So this can't wait until Tuesday."

He sucked in a breath, feeling like his friend had punched him. It was true. Today was her last day. He'd been trying not to think about it. But Miguel had kept asking him questions about the going-away party that Bruno was catering at the end of the day.

The last thing he wanted to do was celebrate her leaving. Throwing her a party was the right thing to do now that he knew the truth. She had landed her dream job. While he didn't want her to leave, he wanted her to be happy. That was why he hadn't told her about his suspicions.

He knew she would be hurt. That she would feel used that he'd seduced her to find evidence against her. So he couldn't tell her.

"I hope like hell you found something to prove she's the damn mole, something we can bring to the police," Ronan said. His face was flushed and his dark eyes glittered with anger.

Simon narrowed his eyes. Usually Ronan was the most laid-back of all of them. "There is no evidence," he assured them.

"There has to be!" Ronan exclaimed.

He shook his head, and he stood because he felt vulnerable sitting with the others standing over his desk. Growing up on the streets, he'd always made certain never to be in a vulnerable position.

Never to sleep with anyone else around…

He'd broken his own rule the other night when he'd slept over at Bette's. He was surprised she hadn't thrown him out after catching his snooping. But she hadn't.

"If there was any evidence against her, I would have found it," Simon assured the others. "She's not the mole."

"Then why is she leaving?" Ronan asked.

"Because she got a better job," he said. "I don't understand why you're all so uptight about this. You're the ones who didn't believe it was her, that she wouldn't be leaving if she'd been making money off us. What's changed?"

Ronan pushed his hand, which was shaking slightly, through his dark hair. "I got reported to the bar for misconduct."

Simon snorted. "So? You've been reported before." With the exception of him, they all had. "What's the big deal?"

"I have a friend at the bar association who looked into it for me," Stone said. "The evidence came from our case files, on our letterhead."

"Damn it!" Simon slammed his fist onto his desk. He was furious that there was a mole in their office. And he was furious that his friends hadn't come to him right away with this latest threat to Street Legal. "Why didn't you guys tell me about this?"

"You've been preoccupied," Trevor said. "With her."

His blood heated as he thought of how preoccupied he'd been—with her crazy, sexy body and their crazy, hot sex. But then it had gotten even crazier than that when they'd shared so much of themselves with each other.

"I was trying to find evidence," he reminded him.

"In her panties?" Ronan crudely asked.

And Simon surged forward, his fists raised. Before he could swing, Trevor caught him, wrapping both arms around him as he pulled him back from Ronan. He wasn't quite as tall or broad as the other guys. But they knew how strong he was.

"You son of a bitch!" he cursed his friend. "Don't talk about her like that!"

Ronan had little respect for women—with good reason, given how his mother had treated his father and how he'd seen other wives treat their husbands. But Bette was different. She wasn't like Ronan's cheating mother.

"Oh, my God," Stone exclaimed, his gray eyes wide with shock. "You're in love with her."

It was a good thing Trevor hadn't let go of him yet. Or he would have swung at Stone, too. "You're fucking nuts!" he said instead. "All of you are. The mole is not Bette."

"Just because you didn't find evidence doesn't mean there isn't any," Stone said, and his voice was lower now, as if he was talking to a child.

Simon glared at him. "I understand that. But she's leaving for a new job."

"With another law firm?" Trevor asked.

"With a fashion house," Simon said. "She's going to have her own line with a major retailer." He would have told him which retailer, but Bette hadn't wanted him to know she designed lingerie so she probably didn't want his partners to know, either.

But Ronan named the retailer.

"How the hell do you know that?" Simon asked. It had taken him nearly two weeks to find out.

"Because Muriel Sanz will be exclusively modeling Bette's Beguiling Bows," Ronan replied, his voice gruff with bitterness.

"Muriel Sanz?" Simon recognized the name of the model and not just because she was famous. "You obliterated her in her divorce."

"She did that to herself," Ronan insisted. "She's a lying, cheating bitch, and I had the witnesses to prove it."

"So what does that have to do with anything?"

"She's the one who reported him to the bar," Stone said, "for the subornation of perjury."

Simon sucked in a breath.

"She and Bette must have cooked up the evidence together," Ronan said, "using our letterhead."

"Anyone in this office could get ahold of our letterhead," Simon pointed out. "Hell, anyone we mailed anything to would have a copy of our letterhead, like Muriel's lawyer. You have nothing connecting Bette to that report to the bar."

"They're friends," Ronan insisted.

With the exception of her former roommate John Paul, and she hadn't introduced them, Simon hadn't met any of Bette's friends. They hadn't had that kind of relationship. It had only been sex.

Would that end today with her last day of work?

Or would she continue to see him if he asked? Or begged? He'd never begged. And he wasn't about to start now. Not even for Bette.

"Just because Muriel is modeling her line doesn't mean they're friends," Simon said. "Not everyone who works together is friends." He wasn't certain how much longer he would be friends with Ronan if the guy continued to bash Bette.

Trevor pulled Simon back a little farther as if he sensed that Simon still wanted to swing.

And Stone cautioned Ronan, "Simon's right. You have no proof that Bette has anything to do with you being reported."

Ronan uttered a ragged sigh.

And Simon felt a twinge of pity for his friend. "The bar will dismiss the report," Simon assured him. "They'll figure out the evidence is fake."

"Then Muriel Sanz will be the one in trouble," Trevor added.

Ronan nodded. But then he stepped closer to Simon and warned him, "Just because we haven't found any proof that Bette's involved doesn't mean that she isn't. You need to be careful."

Simon was afraid that it was already too late for that. But he reminded his friend, "Today is her last day. She won't have anything more to do with Street Legal."

"What about you?" Ronan asked. "Will she have anything more to do with you?"

He shook his head and yet he didn't know. Would she want anything to do with him once she was gone? Or would she be too focused on her new career?

He should have been relieved that she wasn't like all the other women with whom he'd hooked up. She wasn't looking for roses and a ring. She didn't want a future with him or with any other man.

And maybe that was what made her so damn sexy. But hell, he found everything about her sexy. While he couldn't force her to keep working for him, he wasn't ready to let her go completely. Not yet. Maybe not ever...

And that scared him far more than he'd ever been scared in his life.

Simon had given her a heads-up about the going-away party. He'd told her that morning, as they lay in bed together. Since that first night he'd stayed, he'd spent every subsequent night. She should have been freaking out because she felt smothered or overwhelmed. But those weren't the reasons she was freaking out. She was freaking out because she was beginning to expect him to stay.

And she knew that was stupid. No woman held Simon Kramer's interest for very long. She wasn't sure how she'd had him for two weeks. In the two years she'd known him, that was probably the longest he'd dated anyone.

Not that what they were doing was really dating. She wasn't sure what the hell it was, but that she wasn't ready yet for it to end. Would it—once she left Street Legal?

Should she stay?

Not forever. Not even full-time…

But she could help out for a while, make the transition easier for her replacement. Even while she'd been working for Simon full-time, she'd had the time—and maybe the inspiration—to come up with the designs that had become her own line.

But staying, after her going-away party, would be awkward and anticlimactic. No. She had no choice now but to leave Street Legal.

What about Simon?

Should she just end that—whatever it was—too?

Her heart ached at the thought of no longer seeing him, of being with him. Was she in love with him? No. That wasn't possible. She wasn't that stupid.

She drew in a deep, bracing breath and stepped out of her office. Someone called out, "There she is!" Music began to play and confetti rained down on her from some kind of gun Miguel blasted at her.

She blinked against the bits of paper and wished now that she'd worn her glasses. But since Simon had accused her of using them to hide, she only wore them when she was sketching now. Otherwise, she really didn't need them. She also left her hair down, too, which meant it would probably be full of those bits of paper.

But she forced a smile since she was the guest of honor. At least for some. The gossips from the bathroom glared at her with resentment. To them, she was probably the guest of dishonor.

No. Leaving was a smart move. Working with Simon and sleeping with him was stupid. She'd known that when she'd started and couldn't believe it had lasted two weeks. But she was glad now that it had.

She only wished it would last longer.

Sleeping with him...

Not the work.

The gossipy women weren't the only ones glaring at her. A couple of Simon's partners were, as well. Where was Simon? She peered around the crowd of faces but couldn't find him.

With his good looks and charm, he always stood out in any crowd. So he hadn't arrived yet.

Was he coming? Had he authorized the party and

warned her about it only to not attend himself? It made no sense.

"Here's a drink," Miguel said as he pressed a flute of champagne into her hand. "Not that I care to celebrate. I'm really going to miss you."

Warmth flooded her heart. "I'm really going to miss you, too," she said. Despite his past, she'd always felt safe with Miguel—like he had her back and wasn't going to stab it like some of their coworkers. She hugged him.

As he pulled back, he peered over her head. "Guess I'm not the only one who doesn't feel like celebrating," he said. "Simon's not here."

She'd already known that, but a twinge of pain struck her heart with Miguel's confirmation.

"He hasn't even interviewed replacements for you yet," he said. "Of course quite a few current employees have been jockeying for your position."

"I'm sure they have," she said with a sigh.

Miguel squeezed her again before releasing her. "They don't understand you're special to Simon. They will never have the relationship with him that you do."

She wasn't sure what they had could be called a relationship. Yet it was deeper and more meaningful than anything she'd had before.

"You should take the job," she told him. "He can hire someone else for your position."

Miguel tilted his head as if considering it. "I love Simon. But I kind of like being the guy at the door."

That was kind of what he was—the bouncer, allowing people into an exclusive club or throwing them out.

Would he throw her out after today? Would Simon?

"Speaking of which," he murmured as the elevator dinged. He walked off to find out who'd arrived after hours.

Other coworkers replaced him, offering hugs and well-wishes—some sincere, some obviously not. She smiled over how most workplaces were similar to high school. How there were cliques and outcasts in both.

She had never cared to be in the cliques, so she'd been an outcast. But she hadn't minded. She'd used the free time to design. And it had paid off.

"Congratulations," a deep voice murmured.

And she turned to face one of Simon's partners. It was clear from the coldness in Ronan Hall's dark eyes that he wasn't any more sincere in his well-wishes as some of her catty coworkers had been.

"Thank you," she murmured back.

"You've accomplished what no one else ever has," he told her.

Her head began to pound with confusion. "I'm not sure what you're talking about," she admitted. "Plenty of other designers have established their own lines."

She knew Simon was close to his partners, close enough that he would have shared what he'd

how busy she'd been with Simon. What had Muriel done? Not that Ronan didn't have it coming. He'd done far worse to her.

"I don't know what you're talking about," she said as she tugged at her arm.

"Ask Simon," Ronan said. "Ask him why he seduced you. It was to find the evidence that you're the mole."

She'd wondered why he'd suddenly found her attractive after two years of ignoring her. Was this the reason? He'd suspected her of something. Then she remembered all those times he—and his partners—had acted suspicious of her. Her stomach churned, and she felt sick.

That was why he'd searched her apartment. For evidence.

"I am not a mole," she assured him, although she had been called mousy so many times that it had affected her self-esteem. Simon had tried to fix that, though. Or had that only been a con, as well?

Ronan shook his head, refusing to accept her word. "I don't believe you. And I can't believe you convinced Simon that you aren't. You must be damn good."

If he hadn't been holding her wrist, she would have swung at his face. "You son of a bitch!"

"Yeah, I am," he agreed. "That's why a woman like Muriel Sanz or you would never con me the way you've conned Simon."

"Ronan…" It was Stone Michaelsen who spoke to

him. She hadn't even noticed him approach, but he must have been near this entire time. He put his hand over Ronan's on her arm. "You're out of line here."

Ronan shook his head. "I might be out of the bar association because of her and her friend."

Bette looked at Stone and assured him, "I have nothing to do with anything he's been accusing me of."

Ronan snorted in derision. "Yeah, right. Simon was supposed to seduce the truth out of you. And instead you seduced him into believing your lies." He shook his head in disgust.

Simon was supposed to seduce the truth out of you...

Suddenly it all made sense. And she knew Ronan wasn't lying. He was wrong about her being the mole. But he was right about what Simon had done, about why he'd done her.

Pain squeezed her heart so hard that she could barely breathe. Tears burned her eyes so she could barely see. She rushed off, but she wasn't entirely blind. She knew exactly where she was going.

CHAPTER FIFTEEN

SIMON WAS NO HYPOCRITE. He couldn't go out there—
to the party in the lobby—and celebrate her leaving.
Not when he selfishly wanted her to stay. It would
be selfish to expect her to stay here, in a position for
which she was overqualified, just so that he would
get to see her every day just as he had the past two
years.

He'd wasted those two years. Of course he hadn't
wanted to risk a harassment charge. But Bette was
obviously attracted to him, as well.

Wasn't she?

Or had she been conning him like Ronan believed? No. He could not accept that—and not just
because of his ego but because of Bette. She was
not a con.

The door to his office opened and he glanced up
from his desk. His heart flipped in his chest at the
sight of her. She was so damn beautiful, never more
so than now with her hair flowing down her back
and around her shoulders. Bits of colored paper pep-

pered the sleek, sable-colored strands. She closed and locked the door behind her.

And another part of his body leaped to attention, his dick hardening. "Bette…"

He was so damn happy to see her. He stood up and rushed around his desk to her. But as he leaned his head down for her kiss, her hand connected instead of her lips. And his head snapped back with the force of her slap. His skin stung from the blow. "What the hell?"

"What the hell?" she echoed. "How could you think I would betray Street Legal? That I would betray you?"

"What?" he asked. But he knew and he took a step back to sit on the edge of his desk as his legs began to shake slightly beneath him.

"I know why you seduced me," she told him. "That it was just part of your sick plan to get evidence that I'm the office mole."

His phone began to buzz on his desk. He didn't need to read the text to know what had happened but he glanced down at the warning from Stone. "Ronan talked to you."

"Talked?" She made a noise and blinked as if tears were about to sting her eyes. "He accused me of being a con artist, of tricking you and selling out the practice."

"He shouldn't have done that," Simon said.

"Why not? It's what you thought," she said. "I wish you would have just told me that instead of playing games with me, instead of having sex with me." Her face flushed and her eyes gleamed with anger. "That must have been quite a sacrifice for you, sleeping with me in order to get the information you were looking for."

"Sacrifice?" He snorted now. "It was never a sacrifice."

"I know you," she said. "I know you would do anything for this practice. I guess even me."

"Bette…" He'd thought he'd convinced her that she was beautiful and desirable, that he wanted her for her. But that wasn't why he'd started showing an interest in her. And now she knew that. "You know I want you. Even now." He stood up and reached for her, pulling her soft body tightly against his hard, tense one.

Her lips parted on a soft gasp. "Simon…"

"You make me crazy," he told her. And he proceeded to show her just how crazy she made him as he leaned down and covered her mouth with his. He kissed her deeply, sliding his tongue in and out of her open lips. He pushed her back onto the desk, atop his papers and pushed up her skirt.

She didn't fight him. Instead, she locked her legs around his waist and ground her hips against him. She wanted him, too.

He kept kissing her, his mouth making love to hers. But he pulled out a condom as he did it, fumbled with the packet and rolled it over the cock he barely managed to release before it shoved right through his zipper. Then he was inside her—and she was already wet and ready for him, already half coming as her muscles clutched him.

She convulsed around him, squeezing him until he came, too.

"See how crazy you make me?" he asked.

"According to your friend, I've conned you," she said. "Do you believe that?"

"No!" Maybe he'd said it too quickly or maybe he'd hesitated too long. Either way he hadn't answered it correctly because she jerked out of his arms. He reached for her again, but she stepped farther away and jerked down her skirt.

"You don't trust me," she said.

"I don't trust anyone," he told her. "And you know why."

"You trust your friends," she said.

"I grew up with them. I wouldn't have survived if they hadn't been worthy of my trust."

"So you must believe Ronan—about Muriel."

He tensed now. "Is she your friend?"

She nodded.

"Why didn't you tell me that?" And now he was suspicious. Could he have been wrong about her? Had she conned him after all?

"Do I know all your friends?" she asked.

He chuckled. "Yeah, you probably do."

Her face flushed.

"Why didn't you introduce me to any of your

friends?" he wondered. "Were you embarrassed to be dating me?"

He hadn't considered it until now. But it made sense that she might be, considering their practice had hurt one of her friends.

"I didn't know what we were doing," she said. "And I didn't expect it to last as long as it has."

"No," he agreed. "That was why you started it so I would release you early from your two-week notice." So she had conned him. "Was your contract with the fashion house your only reason for leaving Street Legal?"

"No," she admitted. "I don't respect the way you do business. The way you and that PR company obliterated Muriel."

He sighed. It hadn't been pretty. He couldn't deny that. "Ronan had witnesses. He had proof. It was the truth."

She didn't argue that, just replied, "It wasn't fair."

"If you want to win, you can't always fight fair," he said.

"Winning shouldn't be that important," she said. "It shouldn't be at the expense of other people."

"When we win, someone else loses," he said. "That's life, Bette."

"That's your life," she said. "And I don't want any part of it anymore."

He didn't think she was talking about just her job now. "Bette…"

But she wouldn't look at him. Instead she was

looking down at her wrist and the thin gold watch on it. "My two weeks are up," she said. "I never have to see you again."

She didn't have to. But did she want to?

"And Ronan can threaten as much as he wants," she continued, "but he's never going to find any evidence that I'm the mole. I haven't done anything wrong."

He knew he was wrong to have doubted her again, even for a moment. Hell, he'd been wrong to ever doubt her. She was no con artist.

"Except get involved with you," she continued. "That was stupid. I should have known it would bring me nothing but pain."

He had hurt her with his doubts and suspicions. "I'm sorry," he said.

"Why?" she asked. "You won. So it doesn't matter if the other person gets hurt, right?" She must not have cared what he really thought, though, because she didn't wait for his reply. She ran to the door, unlocked and dragged it open, then she ran out of his office.

And out of his life…

So Simon couldn't tell her what he'd just realized. He hadn't won. In fact, for the first time in his life, he'd lost. He'd lost her…forever.

Bette stared down at her sketch pad, but the page was blank. She hadn't felt very inspired the past couple of days, not since she'd run out of Simon Kramer's office and out of Street Legal.

She'd thought maybe coming here—to the fashion house—would inspire her. She was around all the beautiful people since models, photographers and other designers overflowed the old warehouse. But none of those people were as beautiful as Simon. He was really beyond handsome, beyond gorgeous.

And the way he touched her, the way he kissed her...

Heat rushed through her body as tension wound inside her, tension only Simon could fully release. Her vibrator had no effect on her the past couple of nights. She wanted Simon instead.

"Hey, Bette Bow!" a husky, feminine voice called out before slender arms wrapped around her from behind. A head settled onto her shoulder as Muriel Sanz peered down at the sketch pad. "What gorgeous confections are you creating for me to advertise next?"

She tensed in her friend's embrace. And Muriel pulled back. "What's wrong?"

"You should have given me a heads-up," she said, "before you went to the bar association." Then she wouldn't have been so blindsided. But then Simon should have been honest with her about his suspicions, as well.

"I left you some messages to call me back," Muriel reminded her. "You've been MIA since you gave your notice at Street Legal."

She couldn't deny that, but she didn't want to

admit why she'd been. "In one of those voice mails, you could have told me what you'd done."

"You had to know I would go straight to the bar association," Muriel replied, her usually smooth brow furrowed with confusion, "when you gave me those notes."

Bette shook her head, and the pins holding up her hair pulled at her scalp. She wore her glasses, too. But she wasn't hiding anymore, not like she'd done at Street Legal. Her hair was up to get it out of her way. And her glasses were so she could see her sketches...if she ever again summoned the inspiration for a design.

"I did not give you any notes," Bette said. "I don't know what you're talking about—just like I had no idea what Ronan Hall was talking about when he accused me of betraying the firm for my *friend*." Now she wasn't sure how good a friend Muriel really was.

Bette had thought the supermodel was sweet and down-to-earth. But maybe that was just an act. Maybe everything Ronan and that PR firm had said about her was true. She couldn't be trusted.

"Ronan..." Muriel's wide mouth twisted into a grimace of distaste as if just the sound of his name on her lips made her sick. "Of course he would be furious at having his lies exposed."

He was mad. But he'd also been self-righteous. If he'd been lying, would he have felt that way?

Bette didn't know what or whom to believe. She

only knew one thing. "I didn't give you anything," she said. "I had no idea what he was talking about."

Muriel's pale green eyes widened in shock. The light color of her eyes was such a startling contrast to her naturally tanned-looking skin. Her hair was a mass of different-colored streaks of blond, red, brown, gold and black. But it was too random to have been salon styled. The woman had inherited only the best trait of each of the many nationalities making up her heritage. "Those notes really didn't come from you?"

Bette shook her head. "Why did you think they did? Was there a note or anything?" Had someone forged her name? Now she wanted to know who the hell this mole was, too.

"No," Muriel said. "The envelope was just shoved in my box. It wasn't even postmarked. I don't think it had been mailed."

"So someone personally dropped it off?" Bette asked. "What was in it?"

"Notes on Street Legal stationery. Notes about the witnesses and what Ronan had told them to say about me on the stand." She looked sick again, sick of the lies that had been uttered and then spread to ruin her reputation.

But Muriel had risen from the ashes. No matter that it was a lie, she'd started making the most of her bad-girl reputation. And modeling Bette's Beguiling Bows was one of the ways she'd come back into the limelight.

"I can't believe he would do that," Bette murmured.

Muriel gasped. "Do you think those people told the truth about me?"

"No," Bette assured her. Despite her brief moment of doubt, she believed Muriel was a good person. She wasn't the monster her ex-husband and Ronan had made her out to be. "But I can't believe Hall would commit the subornation of perjury and risk his law license."

He, like his partners, had had to overcome so much to become lawyers and build their practice. There was no way that Simon could have known the truth. He cared too much about Street Legal to risk its future.

"He's a bastard," Muriel said. "They all are."

But Bette could not agree with her. She'd seen Simon do good things. He was so patient with his older clients, so supportive of former street kids like Miguel. He was not the bad guy Muriel thought he was. He was not the guy Bette had once thought he was.

She felt a flash of regret over slapping him. But she'd had a good reason. He had seduced her. Too bad she wished that he would do it again.

And again.

But he'd only been doing it—doing her—to find out if she was the mole. He didn't really want her. Like she wanted him.

She had to forget about him and focus on the future she'd fought so hard and for so long to realize. But her pen didn't move across the page. She'd lost her inspiration.

She'd lost Simon.

CHAPTER SIXTEEN

"So what did you think of that one?" Miguel asked from where he leaned against the jamb of Simon's open door.

He glanced up from his desk and focused on his employee, his favorite one now that Bette was gone. He just shook his head.

"She's not Bette?" Miguel wasn't the one who asked this question. Trevor had replaced their male receptionist in the doorway. The two of them were too big to share the space. And Simon could hear the phone ringing at the front desk.

Simon sighed and admitted, "Nobody will be."

"So go get her back," Trevor advised him.

"She has a new job," Simon reminded him. "In the field she always wanted to work in. Hell, she has her own damn line. She's not coming back."

"I didn't mean to the office," Trevor said. "Get her back to you."

Simon shook his head again. "She's damn well not coming back to me, either. Not after Ronan told her

I was only sleeping with her to get evidence against her."

"Ronan was upset," Trevor defended their friend. "He ran his mouth when he shouldn't have."

"He doesn't regret what he said," Simon reminded Trevor. "He still thinks Bette was the mole." Which left them vulnerable to the real mole. But Simon already had some other potential suspects—the women who'd been trying to take Bette's place—in his bed more than her office. He had no intention of seducing the truth out of them, though.

"You don't think she is?" Trevor said.

"I did for a little while," Simon said. "That's why I got close to her in the first place." Why he'd seduced her. He hadn't been able to defend himself against those accusations because they'd been right. Then Bette had defended herself. "But no, she's not the mole."

Trevor nodded. "I trust your judgment."

"Bette will never trust me again," he said. She thought everything had been a con. And they could never build a relationship—a real one—without trust.

For the first time in his life, Simon wanted a real relationship. And for the first time in his life, Simon knew that his charm and his drive wouldn't get him what he wanted.

No matter what he did or said, he wouldn't get Bette back.

* * *

Bette jumped as her doorbell rang. But she shouldn't have been surprised. It was probably Muriel. She lived in the same building and was the one who recommended Bette find an apartment in it. And since she'd learned Bette had nothing to do with those notes from Street Legal, she'd felt so bad over using them that she kept apologizing.

Bette had forgiven her friend. It was Simon whom she couldn't forgive. Sure, he hadn't known her very well when he'd suspected her of betraying the firm. But once he'd gotten to know her, he should have been honest with her. He should have made sure she wasn't blindsided at her own going-away party the way Ronan Hall had blindsided her.

At least she never had to see the sleazy divorce lawyer again.

But then she wouldn't ever see Simon again, either.

Her heart dropped at the thought, hanging low in her chest. She missed him so much, even though she saw him everywhere in the apartment: in the closet, in her bed, in her living room.

She passed through it on her way to the front door. And as she reached for the knob, she allowed herself to hope that when she opened the door, it would be to him. But when she opened the door, Ronan Hall was the man she saw first. He wasn't alone, though. The other two partners from Street Legal stood on either side of him.

Only Simon was missing.

God, she missed him.

"What do you want?" she asked the men. Were they serving her with papers? Suing her for breach of something or other? Not that she'd done anything wrong...

Ronan Hall had been scary mad when he'd confronted her at the party, though. Maybe he'd pressed charges against her or filed a lawsuit.

"We'd like to talk to you." Trevor spoke for the three of them. Usually Simon spoke for the four of them. He was more than the managing partner of Street Legal. He was the gorgeous face of the law practice.

"Talk?" she asked, allowing her skepticism to creep out. "I already told you that I had nothing to do with those notes Muriel sent to the bar association."

At just the mention of the model's name, Ronan's mouth twisted into a grimace of distaste. Hopefully, he wouldn't run into the model on his way out of the building.

She held tightly to the door, prepared to swing it closed in their faces, as she added, "So we have nothing to talk about."

But Stone pressed his palm against the door, holding it open. "Simon. We're here about Simon."

He didn't have to push his way inside then. She hurriedly stepped back to allow them to enter her apartment.

"Simon!" she exclaimed as her pulse quickened with fear. "Is he all right? Has something happened to him?"

He dealt with trusts and wills and such, not the kind of clients or cases the rest of them handled. So she doubted a client had hurt him. But a jealous ex-lover might have. Or some random criminal. He could have been mugged. Or run over on the street.

Her heart pounded fast and fiercely with panic at the thought of all the horrible things that could have happened to him.

The three of them stared at her. So she prodded them, "What is it? What's wrong?"

Ronan sighed. "Damn it."

And more panic clutched her heart. If something had happened to him... "What?" she asked. "What is it?"

"Simon was right," Ronan said, his voice gruff with disappointment. "You're not the mole."

"No, of course not," she said. "While I didn't often agree with how you tried your cases—in the media—I wouldn't interfere. And I wouldn't betray the practice." But most especially, she wouldn't have betrayed Simon. "Now, tell me what's wrong with Simon!"

"You," Ronan replied, but his voice was softer now, his dark eyes warmer. "You're what's wrong with him."

Her head began to pound with confusion. "I don't understand."

"We didn't at first, either," Stone said.

"Speak for yourself," Trevor remarked. "I got it."

Ronan snorted. "Well, I sure as hell didn't. None of us has ever seen him like this."

"Is he hurt?" she asked as concern overwhelmed her. "Is he sick?"

"If I had to guess," Stone began, "and I would have to because I've never felt that way myself, I would have to say that he's heartbroken."

"What?" They were not making any sense. "This is Simon you're talking about? Simon Kramer?"

Ronan nodded as a grin curved up the corner of his mouth. "Yup."

"You broke his heart when you left," Trevor said.

Even as her own heart ached, she laughed. "That's ridiculous. Did you guys come here just to make fun of me?"

"There's nothing funny about it," Ronan said. "He's miserable. And we love him too much to let him continue like this."

"Like what?" she asked.

She couldn't imagine Simon Kramer being miserable. He thrived on adversity and had his entire life. There was nothing and nobody that would or could ever keep him down. Not his own father and not life on the streets.

"He's not eating or sleeping," Trevor said.

Stone added, "He looks like hell."

She narrowed her eyes, skeptical again of their claims. It wasn't possible for Simon Kramer to look like hell. "I doubt that."

"It's true," Trevor agreed.

"And I can't have him looking like that," Stone said, "not when I have a jury trial coming up."

She wasn't certain why or how Simon looked would affect Stone's case, but she didn't ask that. Instead, she asked, "What makes you think his not eating or sleeping has anything to do with me?"

Ronan stepped closer to her and studied her face. "Are you eating or sleeping?"

The dark circles beneath her eyes and thinness of her face provided the evidence he was looking for. She didn't have to answer his question.

But then he asked another. "Do you miss him as much as he's missing you?"

She snorted. "I doubt he's missing me."

"Why do you doubt that?" Stone asked.

"Because Simon Kramer goes after what he wants," she reminded them. "And if he wanted me, he'd be here instead of the three of you."

"That's what makes you different than everyone else," Ronan said as if he'd come to a sudden realization of his own. "You know him. You know him probably as well as we do, and we grew up with him."

Again she wasn't following the lawyer. These guys were brilliant of course, like Simon, but she wasn't stupid. "Yes, I know him, so I know if he was missing me, he'd be here—charming me back into his bed."

Trevor laughed. "It's almost eerie how well she knows him."

"Yes," Stone agreed. "That's why she's scared the hell out of him like no one else ever has."

Ronan nodded. "And we came up against some scary guys on the street. But Simon never flinched until now—until you."

"I don't understand," she admitted.

"When I met Simon, he'd been living on the streets for a while already," Stone said. "He's a little younger than us. Back then he was a lot smaller than us."

"And a hell of a lot prettier," Trevor added.

"Which put him in great danger living on the streets," Stone said. "From other street kids and from adults looking to take sick advantage of runaways like him."

She shuddered, thinking of what could have happened to the man she...

She what?

Before she could answer herself, Ronan was picking up the story. "But Simon wasn't the least bit scared," he said. "He owned those streets and could outsmart everyone else on them."

"Including you," Stone added the verbal jab.

"You, too," Ronan said.

"And he, younger and smaller than us, took care of us," Trevor said.

And she had her answer. She loved him.

"Now we're trying to take care of him," Stone said.

"But I don't understand why he won't come to me

himself," she said, "if he's really missing me." He obviously didn't return her feelings.

"He's scared," Ronan said.

"First time I've ever seen him like this," Stone said. "Maybe it's because he cares more about you than he ever has anyone else. I don't know what it is, but he's scared."

"I hate seeing him like this," Ronan said and all his frustration was back in the gruffness of his voice. It was obviously killing him that he couldn't help his friend. Was he really the monster Muriel thought he was? "And I think you're the only one who can give us back the old Simon."

That was why he was here. She doubted he was convinced that she'd had nothing to do with the information Muriel had received. But for his friend, he was willing to put aside his anger and animosity toward her.

She had always wondered how four alpha dogs worked together without killing each other. It was because they all loved and respected each other. And because Simon was the alpha in charge. His being scared seemed to be scaring them, as well.

But they had no idea what true fear was. She did; it filled her now. It filled her because she knew she loved Simon Kramer. And she wasn't sure what the hell to do about her feelings or about him.

CHAPTER SEVENTEEN

SIMON BLINKED AND tried to focus on his computer monitor. It was late. Or early. He didn't even know. Since Bette's two-week notice had ended, he'd been working around the clock—doing his work and hers. He'd finally brought in a temp, but it was easier to do most of the work than try to teach the new guy, especially when it was so hard for Simon to see anyone else at Bette's desk.

That was why he'd begun doing most of his work before and after the office opened for business. Then he didn't have to see the temp or anyone else for that matter because there was only one person he really wanted to see. But she hated him.

And he could hardly blame her. She undoubtedly felt used and betrayed. That was the part he'd hated most about being a con artist. It was why he'd run away from his father. And when he'd been forced to con people in order to survive on the streets, he'd made certain they never realized he'd conned them, so they wouldn't feel that way.

The way Bette felt…

He wanted to make it up to her, but he didn't know how. Anything he did would just come across as another con to her, as his trying to seduce her again.

Oh, how he wanted to seduce her. His body ached for hers, for the release only she could give him. He could have called any other old girlfriend. Hell, he could have taken up half the office staff on the blatant invitations they'd been issuing since Bette left. But he wanted no one but her. She was the one.

He rubbed his hands over his face. God, he was losing it. He didn't believe in that bullshit soul mate stuff. Hell, he didn't believe in love. But then he'd never felt the way he felt about Bette...

It was new. It was different. Hell, it was love.

He needed a drink. The guys had been trying to get him back to The Meet Market for weeks. Maybe he would call them up and see if they were available. He'd been spending too much time alone, and it was making him lonely, which was something he never was, even when he was alone. Before he could reach for the cell phone sitting on his desk, he heard the ding of the elevator doors opening onto the floor for Street Legal.

Someone was here.

Probably Stone. Or Trevor. Or all three of them. Ronan wouldn't dare come see him alone, not unless one of the other two was available to pull Simon off him. He still wanted to pound the shit out of him for going after Bette, for accusing her of betraying the firm and most of all for telling her that Simon had just been conning her the entire time.

She must have been devastated if she cared about him at all. Did she care?

His heart began to pound fast at the sound of heels tapping across the hardwood floor. The guys didn't wear heels. Half the time they didn't even wear dress shoes. Stone wore boots and Trevor and Ronan wore tennis shoes. It wasn't one of his partners who'd gotten off the elevator. And it certainly wasn't Miguel, who sounded like a train coming when he approached.

But just because whoever had arrived was probably female didn't mean it was Bette. It was probably one of the employees who'd blatantly offered to take her spot in the office and out of it.

Or maybe it was someone else...

He remembered what he'd thought the last time he'd caught someone coming into the office after hours. That he'd caught the mole. He'd been wrong that time. But perhaps this time he would find out who was really betraying Street Legal.

Because while Ronan was wrong about Bette providing that material to Muriel Sanz, someone else from the office definitely might have. He needed to get focused on that again, on discovering who the mole might really be. And he needed to focus on his work. But she was all he could think about at the moment. She was all he could think about every moment of every day.

The tapping stopped right outside his door. But there was a long silence before the knob turned and the hinges creaked as the door opened.

He wasn't armed. Even on the streets he'd never needed a weapon beyond his mind and his mouth. But now he was beginning to wonder if he should carry one. How desperate would the mole be if he or she got caught?

As desperate as Simon was to see Bette again?

Because he imagined she was the one standing in the open doorway. Even though the person's face was in shadow, the silhouette looked like her curvy one. But if she was wearing a skirt and cardigan, it was covered by an overcoat with the belt bound tightly around her small waist.

His pulse quickened. And while he was more afraid than he'd ever been, he knew he didn't need a weapon.

If this was Bette, he had no way of protecting himself from her. The visitor stepped forward into the light cast by the lamp on his desk. And his heart slammed against his ribs.

It was Bette. Her hair was piled on top of her head. But it wasn't tightly bound. And she wasn't wearing her glasses, either. Her long, thick lashes fluttered freely as she blinked and looked at him as if she couldn't believe her eyes.

He ran his hand over his face again and felt the stubble. He'd forgotten to shave today. Maybe yesterday, too.

Damn, he probably looked like hell.

She continued to stare at him as if she barely recognized him. He couldn't stop looking at her, either, but because she was so damn beautiful. The most beautiful woman he'd ever seen...

"Where are they?" she asked.

He cocked his head. "Who? It's after hours. Everybody's gone for the night."

"The flowers," she said. "The past two years I sent flowers to every single one of your flings when you ended it with them. But I didn't get any flowers."

"I didn't end it," he reminded her. "I wouldn't have ended it."

Ever.

The thought shocked him, but it didn't scare him now, like it had when he'd first acknowledged that he had real feelings for her and they weren't going away even though she had.

"I still would have liked some flowers," she said.

He gestured at the paperwork on his desk. "I don't have any."

She sighed. "Then I guess you'll have to make it up to me another way."

He sucked in a breath. "Any way you'd like." *In the chair, on the desk.*

But he wasn't pushing his luck, so he didn't suggest any of those things. "What would you like?" he asked her.

"An opinion."

He hadn't expected that, so he arched a brow in question. She walked closer and ran a fingertip over his brow.

"I've missed that," she murmured and her lips curved into a small, wistful smile.

"I've missed you," he admitted, his voice deep and gruff with the emotion rushing over him. "I've missed you so damn much."

Her smile widened, and her breath shuddered out as if she was relieved. And happy...

"So you're glad that I've been miserable without you?" he asked. "That I've missed you so much that I haven't been eating or sleeping?"

"Yes," she answered.

"And the only reason you've come to see me tonight is for an opinion?" he asked, hoping to prod her into making the same admission he just had.

That she missed *him*, that she needed *him*.

But she just nodded and reached for the belt of her overcoat. She undid the belt, then shrugged off the jacket so that it dropped onto the floor around her feet. She wore one of her designs beneath the coat. It had to be hers because it was adorned with those damn beguiling bows.

It was a braless corset that was more satin ribbon than material. The ribbon zigzagged through a thin piece of blue silk which must have had enough starch to it to boost her breasts up so they were even higher and fuller than usual.

His breath escaped in a hiss while his cock hardened and pulsed. "Damn..." he murmured.

She twirled around, showing off the back, which was all ribbon and bows, as well. "You don't like it?"

He stood up so quickly and abruptly that his chair toppled over. Then he reached for her, jerking her up against his body. "No," he told her.

Her bottom lip, with that little crease in the middle of the fullness, poofed out in a pout. "You don't? I was thinking about using this for the line…"

"I don't like it," he said. "I love it."

But that wasn't all he loved. With his hands on her bare, silky shoulders, he eased her away from him. Then he reached for one of the bows, his fingers trembling slightly as he tugged on it. The ribbon stayed in place. And he narrowed his eyes in frustration.

She laughed. "You didn't think I was going to make it easy for you, did you?"

He shook his head. "Not you…"

She would always be a challenge to him. She would never bore him.

"You're going to have to keep trying until you find the right bow," she said, "before you'll see me naked."

"Will I see you naked?" he wondered. "Even if I get this thing off you? Will I see you really naked?" Because that was what he wanted. He wanted to know Bette in the way that she'd gotten to know him. Completely.

He was asking for more than her body. For more than sex…

And for the first time in her life, Bette was ready

to give herself completely to someone else. She wasn't worried anymore that she would wind up like her mom or sister. She knew she wasn't like them. And Simon was definitely not her father or brother-in-law. He wouldn't expect her to give up anything for him.

"I missed you," she said, her breath escaping in a ragged sigh. "So damn much."

"I'm sorry," he said. "I should have told you about my suspicions."

She smiled. "But what if I had been the mole? You would have tipped me off."

"You're not the mole. I figured that out pretty damn fast," he admitted. "But I wanted to keep seeing you, keep being with you."

"I wanted to keep seeing you," she said. "Keep being with you. I even considered offering to stay on part-time as your assistant."

He shook his head. "As much as I hated you leaving, I wouldn't want you to stay. This isn't the job for you. Being a fashion designer, that's what you love."

And he was whom she loved. More than she'd thought it possible to love anyone.

"Before I could offer," she reminded him, "Ronan confronted me about Muriel."

He lifted his hand from the satin ribbon to her face, his palm gently cupping her cheek. "You should be the model," he murmured. "These designs aren't just made *by* you, they're made *for* you."

She shook her head. "You are the only one I want

seeing *me* in them." She drew in a deep breath, bracing herself, before admitting, "You're the only one I want to see me naked." She tugged on the right bow, the one that had the corset dropping away from her body. "Really naked."

He tensed and stared at her face, his blue eyes wide with hope. "Bette."

"I have really fallen in love with you."

He laughed and wrapped his arms around her. "It's about damn time!" he said. "I have loved you for so long!"

She snorted at his claim. "Not very damn long," she said. "You ignored me for two years."

He shook his head. "I tried to ignore you," he said. "But I never should have hired you in the first place. You have no experience or education to work in a law firm."

She eased back and studied his face. "That's true. So why did you hire me?"

"Because I wanted to see you every day," he said. "Even if I couldn't touch you, I wanted to see you."

"You can touch me now," she said.

Now he stepped back and looked at more than her face. He looked at her body. And his breath hissed out between his clenched teeth.

"You are so damn beautiful."

She didn't argue with him or doubt him. She knew it was true. And she felt beautiful. "Thank you."

He grinned. "Thank *you*."

"I haven't done anything yet." But she reached for the zipper of his pants.

He caught her hand in his and held it still in his gentle grasp. "You came here," he said. "I was afraid to come to you."

"If your friends hadn't told me that, I probably wouldn't have found the courage to come," she admitted.

"My friends? The guys came to you?"

She nodded.

"Assholes," he murmured. But he was grinning as he said it. "Now I'm going to have to thank them, too."

"Hopefully, not like you're going to thank me," she said.

He laughed as he reached for her. Swinging her up in his arms, he carried her to the couch. After he laid her on the supple leather, he stood up. And again he just stared at her, his blue eyes dark with passion and something else.

Something she recognized now as love. She'd wondered before how she would be able to know for certain what someone else was feeling. She would never have to wonder with Simon. She could see the love in his eyes.

She lifted her arms, holding them out for him. But before he joined her, he shrugged off his suit jacket and unbuttoned his shirt. Then he finished lowering his zipper and kicked off his shoes and the pants and his briefs. Finally, he was naked, too.

As naked as she was.

But he didn't join her on the couch. He knelt on the floor beside her, like he was worshipping her body. And he made her feel that way, with his gentle touch. He glided his fingertips along her shoulder, down her arm to the curve of her hip. He traced her entire silhouette as if he was trying to memorize the shape of her.

"You are perfect," he said.

She would have teased him for laying it on a little thick. But she saw in his eyes that he was sincere. To him, she was perfect.

Love for him overwhelming her, she reached out. She traced the line of his broad shoulders and the muscles in his arms and chest. Then she tried to move lower, to slide her mouth over his pulsating shaft and take him deep in her throat.

She was pulsating, too, her body quivering as the tension he'd built inside her became overwhelming. "Please, Simon," she implored him. "I need you."

"I need you, too," he assured her.

But he didn't hurry. He took his time. Lowering his head to hers, he kissed her gently, his lips just whispering across hers.

She gasped at the sensation, and he dipped his tongue inside her mouth. She suckled on it like she wanted to suck on him. And he groaned. Then his hands moved to her breasts, molding the flesh, teasing the nipples.

She whimpered as that need became unbearable.

Tears of frustration stung her eyes. Then finally he touched her core, and she came apart.

It wasn't enough, though. She needed him inside her.

Plastic crinkled as he tore open a condom packet. His hand shook as he rolled it on, then he lifted her onto his lap where he knelt on the floor beside the couch.

She locked her legs around his back as she bounced and rocked, sliding up and down his shaft. He teased her nipples, then he reached between them and rubbed his thumb over her mound, finding the most sensitive part of her.

She cried out as she came again.

And he stood, with her locked yet around his waist, with him buried deep inside her. And he arched his hips up, making love to her standing up. Until his legs began to shake.

Then finally he yelled her name and his body shuddered as he came, too. They collapsed onto the couch where they'd had sex for the first time. This time it hadn't been just sex, though. They'd made love—because they had really fallen for each other.

She smiled, and he must have felt her cheek move against his chest from where she'd settled in his arms. He smiled, too.

"This feels so damn right," he murmured.

"Yes, it does," she agreed.

"You and me," he said. "The fashion designer and the lawyer."

They might not have been the likeliest combination. But she was certain they would make it work because they respected each other, respected how hard each other had worked to accomplish what they had. But what Simon had worked so hard to achieve was in jeopardy now.

"Do you have any idea who the mole really is?" she asked him.

The smile slid away from his mouth. "No."

"You'll figure it out," she assured him. He was the smartest man she'd ever met. "And I'll do whatever I can to help you."

He tightened his arm around her shoulders, holding her more snugly against his chest. "This helps," he assured her. "Just having you here."

"In your office?" He didn't actually expect her to come back, did he? She'd liked that he hadn't wanted her to sacrifice her dreams for his.

As if he felt her tension, he stroked his hand down her back and assured her, "I told you that I want you to focus on your passion."

She smiled.

"And you're mine. That's what I meant about having you here—in my arms." He chuckled. "In my heart, too, Bette Monroe."

"You're in my heart, too," she assured him because she knew how hard it was to be so vulnerable, how scary it was.

But Simon didn't seem scared anymore. He seemed happy. "Loving you has put things in perspective for me," he continued. "The practice isn't everything to me anymore. You are."

She sucked in a breath, surprised by just how vulnerable he'd made himself to her. He was so damn brave.

"It's okay if you don't feel the same way," he assured her. "I know your designs—working as hard as you have to get your own line—mean everything. And they should—"

"They mean more because of you," she said. "They mean more because you understand and support me. While I haven't always agreed with the way Street Legal has handled cases, I understand and support you, too."

He grinned now. "And that's everything."

She had to agree that it was—whatever they had, it was so special, so unique. "And you're everything to me," she assured him.

He released a breath she hadn't realized he'd been holding. As if he'd needed that assurance from her.

He needed her as much as she needed him. They were equals—in their lives and in each other's hearts. Bette knew now that she'd achieved the goals she'd always had, the ones she'd admitted to herself and the one she hadn't even realized she'd had until she'd applied for the job as Simon Kramer's assistant. She'd wanted him to fall in love with her.

And she was glad that she'd fallen for him, too.

* * * * *

LET'S TALK
Romance

For exclusive extracts, competitions
and special offers, find us online:

- **f** facebook.com/millsandboon
- **⊙** @millsandboonuk
- **𝕏** @millsandboon

Or get in touch on 0844 844 1351*

For all the latest titles coming soon, visit
millsandboon.co.uk/nextmonth